DUENNA TO
A MURDER

DUENNA TO A MURDER

RUFUS KING

WILDSIDE PRESS

Published by Wildside Press LLC.
www.wildsidepress.com

The corpse had been a man of considerable physical charm. His body lay face down on the gravel drive of Brandgwyn in the small sea-coast town of Parnellton. Dusk of a South Carolina evening lingered, hazily exposing a thin feather of smoke from a cigar lying just beyond the reach of limp fingers, and the dusk showed, too, a dark seepage of blood from a throat wound which had stabbed the jugular vein. This was the evening of Saturday, June twelfth.

CHAPTER 1

"Mr. Harden will see you now, Mrs. Tyler."

Harden's secretary held the door open, and Melissa Tyler went into a room which seemed less to her like an office than the lounge in a small and exclusive club. A sexless one. Harden, over at the desk, gave up examining an antiquated coffee mill and a woman's elbow-length scarlet glove. He stood and came to meet her. He was a compact man, philosophically accepting a retreating hairline, and with a face that had been trained as a sympathetic mirror for anything from the simple to the exorbitant, and certainly for the grotesque.

"Good morning, Mrs. Tyler. Rotten day. Do you ever get it like this down in Parnellton?"

Melissa looked at rain sheeting eastward across New York and running drearily down windowpanes.

"As I remember it, we do, Mr. Harden."

"Oh? I thought you had always lived there."

"No, I left Parnellton twenty years ago. We've been back just a month." Melissa took the chair he held for her. "A long month, Mr. Harden."

"I see. Well, suppose you tell me about it, and let me know what we can do."

"I understand that you"—for a moment Melissa sifted words—"that your organization does do anything?"

"In a very broad sense, yes. Take this coffee mill. The client wanted one contemporaneous with her 1830 Boardman pewter pot. It took sixty-nine attics before we landed it over in Berks County, Pennsylvania. We had much less trouble over a Cambrian fossil."

Melissa smiled back doubtfully.

"It isn't—I mean there's no shopping connected with it. Do you handle more personal, more complex things?"

"Complexities are our main source of income, Mrs. Tyler."

Jake Harden was accustomed to these initial skirmishes and had developed an enormous patience. The wants of most clients were clearly defined, no matter how bizarre, but many dealt in intimate equations with a resultant natural reluctance at discussing them with a stranger—such as that recent assignment involving a visiting potentate's wife who had had a naive if diplomatically embarrassing leaning toward arson.

Jake observed Melissa Tyler while waiting for her to plunge. He was satisfied with the expensiveness of her getup, from the angle of fees, but it puzzled him too. Summer sables draped a dress of Egyptian-green wool that had all the earmarks of a top custom-made job. The accessories, the hat, all had a new, a just-out-of-the-bandbox look. This was all right, but the bother was that they looked unaccustomed to Melissa Tyler, as though only this instant they inexplicably had landed on her.

To a measure he understood this when she said: "Mr. Harden, I have recently inherited a great deal of money. My cousin, a Miss Elizabeth Brandgwyn, left me her estate. She held considerable business interests and a good deal of property in Charleston—Parnellton is just north along the coast from Charleston. The executors have just finished settling things, and the amount goes into a good many millions. They've been very kind. Even during the past month, before the estate became technically mine, they placed an absurdly large drawing account at my disposal."

"Absurdly large, Mrs. Tyler?"

"For us, very. We were poor. I don't mean poverty-stricken or anything like that, but we had to live carefully and run our home in Los Angeles so that everything counted. Henry, my husband, has tried so hard to be successful, and every cent we could spare above living expenses was used for Francine."

"Your—daughter?"

"Yes, our only child. She sings."

"Would it be in connection with mapping her career that you've come to see me?"

"Partly so, yes. It's awfully complex. Do you know the south at all, Mr. Harden? Its old families?"

"No, but I imagine most old families in any locality have the same bunch of reactions, if I can guess what you're driving at."

"You're thinking of the inheritance. It isn't entirely money, although the other relatives do resent it. Primarily it's the cold and courteous decision they've reached still to consider me an outcast because I married Henry."

Jake would have liked to know just what sort of a bird Henry had been, and obviously still must be, but Mrs. Tyler simply left her husband in the general pool reserved for the *déclassé*—he could be anything from an ex-crook to a blatant and obviously unfashionable mental case. Melissa, at last having started, went on.

"There was a good deal of publicity when Miss Brandgwyn died, and after the terms of her will were known. It was picked up by the Los Angeles papers and they treated it pretty outrageously, Mr. Harden—turning me into a middle-aged Cinderella or a from-rags-to-riches sort of thing. Any number of reporters came to see us. They wrote articles about Francine's voice and some horrid things about Henry and—well, I imagine you know Los Angeles."

"Cranks, crooks, begging letters, swamis? You began to be hit with the works?"

"Yes, and some of it is still going on. That's one of the things I'd like, someone to act as a buffer, almost even as a protection."

"Were there threats?"

"Several. I took them to the district attorney in Los Angeles, and he assured me, quite rightly, that under the circumstances I must expect them. He considered them merely as the work of cranks and not as being actively dangerous. He suggested my turning them over to the postal authorities, which I did."

"Did they trace any of them down?"

"Yes, a few. Just cranks, feeble-minded, harmless—they assured me it would keep up until after the publicity died down. They suggested that I engage a private investigator if it worried me too badly, but it was evident they didn't think it necessary."

"Did you?"

"No, because I wanted something more than just a detective. I'd like someone who can handle the letters with good judgment and with tact, and to keep us out of possible trouble. I suppose I'm looking for both the impossible and the ideal."

"Not at all. We can take care of it, Mrs. Tyler."

"And Francine?" Melissa's gloved hands clenched perceptibly as she added: "Mostly Francine, Mr. Harden."

"You're not speaking of her career now, are you?"

"No. It's something I don't know, but I know it's there. In some fashion it involves two men, and, frankly, I'm nervous about it. A tactful person, an outsider, might find some suggestion as to what is at the bottom of it. Children just don't confide in their parents about some of their troubles. I didn't. I imagine you didn't."

"That's right."

"Well, those are the reasons why I'm here. I'd like you to assign one of your assistants to come back with me and stay in Parnellton until things straighten out."

Jake appreciated that such things as Melissa Tyler was holding in reserve would show up later. He was convinced of their existence and their serious nature, serious enough to a point where they were worrying her badly. If they showed signs of becoming criminally threatening to her, he would suggest having the assignment transferred to the proper officials.

"How old is your daughter, Mrs. Tyler?"

"Nineteen."

Jake glanced at a desk calendar. Thursday, June third.

"Miss Gilland will be best for your problem. Margot Gilland. She ties up her present job this evening and can take you on tomorrow. She is twenty-two, which is close enough to your daughter's age to be of help in establishing some willingness toward confidences. Her family background's in the diplomatic corps. Lost her fiancé during that courageous mess at Tarawa. So she threw herself into becoming a career woman, and I'm afraid she will be. May heaven help her." Jake smiled warmly. "Don't let that throw you, Mrs. Tyler. Miss Gilland still has a few traces left of being almost human."

CHAPTER 2

The coast town of Parnellton had the customary languorous physical attributes of the low country. It was seasonally odorous with jasmine and magnolias, brazen with the fulsomeness of its well-publicized azaleas, and atmospherically sinister with its omnipresent shredded-shrouds effect of Spanish moss.

Its population proper were employees of the furniture works where cypress wood was fashioned into garden and patio pieces of artistically rigid discomfort. There were the outlying plantation houses, for the most part tenanted by end-of-the-line descendants who were putting the best face possible on a dispiriting indigence. Otherwise the town's sole claim to notability lay in its inn.

This inn, the Wynstable, had been opened forty years ago as a distinguished and frighteningly expensive retreat for convalescents. Its policy was dedicated purely to the therapeutic values of utter rest. This both relieved it from any medical kickbacks and cut down on the overhead handsomely.

Any sport more fervid than the kindlier versions of lawn croquet was frowned upon. Quiet tables at cards were approved. A trio composed of a restrained pianist, a violin, and a cello painstakingly dissected dinner music of a ripened age on Saturday nights.

Through the years the original building, with its tiers of shade-giving piazzas fronting on the bay, had increased its guest capacity by the gradual addition of a series of restfully appointed cottages which were serviced from the inn itself. The rate for these antiseptic havens was sixty dollars a day—no reduction for occupancy by the week or month.

Melissa, Henry, and Francine Tyler occupied one of them.

This occupancy had not been permitted without a struggle on the part of Mrs. Effingdon Frosher, who had despotically run the place for the past ten years. Mrs. Frosher was an imposing woman, unpadded, and with eyes which protruded slightly in the manner so fashionable among noblewomen of the early French and English courts.

She brooked no nonsense, and any deviation from a palatable appearance of lineage was definitely down in her book as nonsense. Rather the camel through the needle's eye than that a person tinged with the gauche, the common, or the *déclassé* could appear upon the Wynstable's impeccable register.

Melissa Tyler had put her on a spot. Melissa had shown up a month ago and simply said that she and her husband and her daughter would stay at the inn until the technicalities of her cousin's will were settled, when they would install themselves at Brandgwyn. This would have been all right with Mrs. Frosher, because Melissa was after all a Brandgwyn, but she was also a Tyler and he was with her. Francine apparently rested in a genealogical state of suspension somewhere in between.

Mrs. Frosher knew pretty nearly all there was to know about Henry Tyler. Parnellton and a good part of South Carolina knew it too. A penitent, well-bred defaulter, even an aristocratically motivated murderer, could have been stomached by the county no matter how indigestibly, especially had his crime been one of chivalrous passion.

But you could not stomach a carnival knife thrower, which Henry was, and a (worse) tattooed man, which Henry also was. As a clincher, it was common knowledge that Henry had exhibited the decorative effects of his torso *et al* on innumerable midways with a positively abandoned gusto.

For years it had been locally accepted with a sympathetic tolerance that the late Miss Elizabeth Brandgwyn, in spite of her acute business acumen, had been in the habit of indulging a few off-the-main-line conceits. An appetite for flying box kites had been one of them. Another had been a delusion that she was a coloratura in the great tradition of Tetrazzini. This latter felony had been upsetting in that it had involved bleak soirees attended by weak-willed friends upon whose eardrums, accompanied by a flute player, it had pleased her to prove her contention.

In view of these oddities, it had not come as any blistering surprise to the rest of the Brandgwyn clan when Miss Elizabeth left her potfuls of wealth to the distant Cousin Melissa with her walking-picture-salon, dagger-hurling Henry. The loot had been wrapped up, incidentally, in an unbreakably ironclad last will and testament.

All of this knowledge still had not solved Mrs. Frosher's dilemma. True, Miss Elizabeth was dead, but her hair-raising fortune, as well as a good dose of Brandgwyn blood, was very much alive in Melissa Tyler, and Melissa had every intention of enjoying the spoils of this wealth from Brandgwyn. Also, Mrs. Frosher had no doubts, its power.

A conclusively harassing note was the fact that the Wynstable grounds were a part of the Brandgwyn plantation on a long-term lease.

The cankerous upshot was that Mrs. Frosher had installed the Tylers in the most outer-flung of the inn's cottages. She had done this in the dismal hope that through some great beneficence of chance Henry would stay cooped up in it, somewhat like the prisoner of Zenda, and which of course he didn't.

It had definitely been the roiled state of mind into which Melissa had plunged her that had caused Mrs. Frosher so unquestioningly to inscribe as guests on the Wynstable register a Mrs. Penelope Millay (convalescent, widow) and Forrest Millay (son). The Millays had appeared on the same day as the Tylers' tainted arrival, and due to her momentary headlessness, Mrs. Frosher had omitted completely her customary checkup in the nation's Social Registers and Who's Who.

She had assigned the Millays to the only cottage which then had been vacant. It neighbored on Melissa's, and Mrs. Frosher clutched a wraithlike hope that Mrs. Millay's convalescence would not experience too noticeable a setback from any ornamental view of Henry in, say, a pair of swim trunks.

The risk of chancing this unprepared-for glimpse of a totally tattooed fellow guest had suddenly seemed unwise, and so, to a measure, Mrs. Frosher had explained how things stood.

"I hope you don't mind," she had said.

Mrs. Millay, whose face beneath its raddled appearance both of age and of a conquered illness held a dignity and certain charm, had been reassuring.

"Not at all, Mrs. Frosher. I'm afraid I have lived too long either to be startled or shocked by anything."

CHAPTER 3

In spite of Jake Harden's dim viewpoint on women who head at a brittle clip into careers, Margot Gilland successfully kept under wraps the more outwardly recognizable mannerisms of the type. Her conversation did not reduce her less in-the-know listeners to the status of dumb doras being sniped at with palsey celebrities, open-armed *maître d's* of impregnable huddle joints, and a pronunciation of certain common words which was so correct that nobody but Webster would believe it.

Her dress subtly by-passed both the cleverly tailored uniform-in-black as well as any *dernier cri* in high fashion which would be so utterly *dernier* as to startle her less sensational sisters into a decline, brought on by the horrid suspicion that they looked like animate grain bags.

She collected a good deal of Parnellton background from Melissa Tyler during their flight down to Charleston on Friday, June fourth— the day following Melissa's interview with Jake. A thumbnail sketch of Henry Tyler was gathered in, too, but there remained a haze of enigma still shrouding Francine.

Melissa concentrated pretty exclusively on Francine's background of voice study. This, during Francine's childhood, had been of a catch-as-catch-can nature due to Henry Tyler's job.

"We were always on the move," Melissa said. "Francine and I, of course, traveled with the shows. I just had to be with Henry."

Margot gauged the larger picture which Melissa's capsule remark covered: Melissa's lunge from the deadly dull and threadbare ritualism of a moribund society into the arms of Henry, no matter how pictorially coated, had not been just a flare of passion but a lasting thing.

Later on, Melissa said, Henry had given up carnivals, and he had done it for Francine's sake. He had retired his billings of "*Cokaine—the Mad Apache of Paris, France* under which in a Breton jersey, baggy pants, and a beret he had hurled his knives, and of "*Michael Angelo—Not an Inch Unadorned*," as whom, garbed in truly nothing to speak of, he had displayed his artistic patina.

They had settled in Hollywood, where they established the most precarious sort of a toe hold in order that Francine, who was by then sixteen years old, might have as good a training for her voice as they could afford. It was little enough. Henry had fed and housed them as well as he could through the fitful work of an extra in the movies, with occasional better-paying windfalls when any doubling as a dagger hurler might be in demand.

Cousin Elizabeth had visited them for a week during this Hollywood period. She had got on awfully well with Henry, to whom she had divulged some of the finer points of box-kite flying. In return, and with no notable success, he had led her through a beginner's step or two in the technique of so throwing a knife that it would land within some approximate yardage of its intended target.

She had made no gesture toward underwriting Francine's career, and her bread-and-butter gift to Melissa had been financially modest: a linen luncheon set printed with trained seals. So naturally it had come as a staggering shock to Melissa when, a year later, she had found herself swamped under the load of Elizabeth's millions.

As for Francine's future, Melissa said she now thought it best to go slow, a course pleasantly possible in view of all financial strains having been lifted. She wanted Francine to perfect an absolute technical foundation before attempting any significantly important debut.

A few minor public appearances now and then, yes, to build up platform confidence—in fact, Melissa said, arrangements already had been made with the Charleston chapter of a Southern women's organization for a recital one week from tomorrow, for Saturday, June twelfth. The recital was to be a benefit performance for one of the city's historical (and disintegrating) houses.

The sponsoring organization impressed Margot, for she knew its reputation of being ultraconservative and hidebound by social tradition. In view of the cold front erected against Melissa because of Henry, it seemed curious that they would sponsor Francine even on a professional basis.

She said so, and Melissa said: "They never would have, only Anne Calverse insisted. She suggested the recital in the first place and persuaded Francine, and then she made an awfully strong issue of it at the club. She's the president."

"But why, Mrs. Tyler?"

"I think because of Cousin Elizabeth, for one thing. They were terribly fond of each other, in spite of their difference in age. And because of Bruce. He's Anne's son."

"How does he enter it?"

Suddenly, frighteningly, right there in the plane, Melissa burst into tears. It took Margot and the stewardess several minutes to quiet her, with Margot smiling understandingly at the politely incurious passengers and murmuring: "Nerves—just an attack of nerves."

Later, calmly, Melissa explained. Stripped of any embellishments, it amounted to Mrs. Calverse having been the sole member of the old guard to have called on the Tylers at the Wynstable and to offer Melissa the hand of friendship. She had brought her son Bruce with her, and Bruce and Francine had fallen in love with that unreasoning swiftness and intensity which frequently can and does occur.

"There's a violence in Southern men," Melissa said.

She expanded the point, and Margot gathered that in addition to his animal strength and lowering dark good looks Bruce Calverse possessed almost more than his proportionate share of this stormy regional attribute.

"Francine felt just as deeply as Bruce did, Miss Gilland, and that's why I simply cannot understand it."

It seemed that this love, this swamping passion, had been bleaked out just as swiftly as it had sprung into being. In fact, after but one broiling week of existence Francine had extinguished it—with Bruce Calverse, inferentially, still left whizzing along under a full head of violent Southern steam.

Well, that was it. Francine had coldly, and with what appeared to be the most heartless sort of capriciousness, just thrown Bruce over. Not that that was all. With an even greater show of heartlessness, she immediately had begun to flaunt a disgraceful, really a brazen amount of interest in a young man who, with his convalescing mother, was occupying the cottage which adjoined theirs at the Wynstable.

His name was Forrest Millay.

Melissa insisted there was no shred of sense to any of it. It ran counter to everything that was decent and good and kind in Francine's nature. Her character was too fine even to admit of such an act, and yet that was how things stood.

Both Melissa and Henry had tried to get some logical or even some temperamentally emotional explanation from Francine, but she had defiantly clammed up and had withdrawn behind an unnaturally hard-boiled manner which plainly had hurt them very much.

"Francine means just about everything there is in life to us," Melissa said. She looked miserable and as though she were going to cry again. "I feel awfully sure she is still in love with Bruce, Miss Gilland."

This three-ring circus of the affections did not impress Margot nearly so much as the fact that the recital, under Anne Calverse's sponsorship, should still be on the books—in spite of Francine's all-but-guttersnipe brush-off to the Calverse son-and-heir.

There was something strong about that fact, and it wasn't good.

Margot had her first view of Henry when he met them at the airport. He had successfully carried the flat athleticism of his youth into the early forties. None of his shock of sepia hair had vanished, and such experimental lines as had encroached upon his face only added to its strength.

His coat of tan was of a long-established, lively mahogany. On it, at the base of his throat where a white sports shirt triangled upward, Margot noted with an uncontrollable fascination the ultramarine head of a tattooed cobra which was flanked on either side, for some doubtlessly tasteful reason, by a starchy pair of American flags.

His smile, his handclasp, both were warmly friendly.

"I'm glad you're here, Miss Gilland. We've needed you."

He drove them through the city with its architectural contradictions between harsh, modern utility and the sprinkling of fine-lined, chimney-potted old houses and an occasional walled garden lovely with magnolia trees. The air released a fragrance of tea olive whenever a lessening of hot, swirling dust would permit.

They picked up Francine at a house on East Bay Street where her present voice teacher was living in a frustrated condition of semi-retirement. He was a Signor Vincente Castelaronni, and his past stable of pupils had, in addition to Miss Brandgwyn's, included larynxes of a caliber comparable to Mary Garden's.

Margot attempted a swift size-up of the girl as Francine walked toward the car: the good diaphragm of a singer—her father's sepia hair shot with undertones of fire, and worn in a defiantly obsolete asbestos-curtain bang over sultry eyes—lips which offered a suggestion of nervous strain and which were painted a raw blood red—a good figure, tensely vital under a simple and hideously expensive dress of lime-colored cotton.

She greeted Melissa with an almost urgent, hungry affection, and Henry said to her: "How did it go today?"

"It didn't. He was drunk as a pig over a letter from some wilted old flame in Salerno. Said she'd written that she was down to her last yard of spaghetti. He busted out bawling in the middle of 'Mon Coeur S'Ouvre à Ta Voix' and just about drowned himself to death."

"I thought it was meant to make people bawl."

"Not the way I was wrecking it."

"This is Miss Gilland."

Francine's acknowledgment was considerably less than cordial. Margot appreciated that a good lump of wary hostility lay beneath the girl's politely surfaced How-do-you-do. As a matter of fact, it was conspicuous enough to amount to the throwing down of a challenging gage.

CHAPTER 4

That evening, in the privacy of a telephone booth adjacent to the Wynstable's somnolent lounge, Margot got in touch with Jake at his New York apartment. She used a dial instrument, to prevent the call from filtering through the inn switchboard operator's antenna-type ears.

She told Jake there was something which she felt their Los Angeles branch should look into. She gave him the address of the house which the Tylers had occupied out on 150th Street just off Central Avenue, as well the address on La Brea near Pico Street where Francine's voice teacher, a Madame Destina Vesturi, had her studio.

"Ask them to look up Francine's contacts there, will you, Jake?"

"Won't she open up?"

"No, she's completely on the defensive. I thought that some background information possibly could be used as a lever."

"I'll get them to put Jaffries on it. What seems to be the trouble?"

"Well, she's got herself in an emotional mess with two men down here, and she's a frightened girl, no matter how hard she tries to cover it up. One of the men is from Cleveland and ought to be checked on. The name is Millay. He's registered here at the inn with his widowed mother, a Mrs. Penelope Millay. His first name is Forrest."

"Bank robbers?"

"Possibly, but very civilized ones. Mrs. Millay must be well off or they couldn't afford to stay here. Anyhow, after rather insultingly jilting a local scion, Francine at once showed a feverish interest in this Millay number. He is, incidentally, a blond Adonis with rugged, pale molasses curls and the build of a practicing pole-vaulter. He blew my brains out when we met this afternoon."

"Sounds irresistible to me. You can scarcely blame Francine."

"I know, but the transfer was too out of character. The Millays' address in Cleveland is the Wade Park Manor."

"And an irreproachable one, if ever. I'll have Davis look them up. What does Millay do, if anything?"

"It seems to be if anything. I think Mrs. Millay has the money. He does hint at an interest in photography and seems headed for some sort of career along that line, in a silver-spoon sort of way. His war background was Navy. I wish Davis would look it up, and also Mrs. Millay's financial rating."

"He will. By the way, what's the low-down on Henry Tyler being a social leper? It's been giving me insomnia trying to guess."

"He's an ex-carnival knife thrower and a completely unex-tattooed man. We took a swim this afternoon and it was like floating around with the Whitney Museum."

"So that was it."

"Yes. I like him."

"I'd like him too. As a pal it would be hard to think of having a more absorbing conversation piece. Look, Margot, aside from the acrobatics of love's young dream, how does the setup strike you in general?"

"I can tell you better after we're settled. We're moving over to the plantation house tomorrow. It's just a short walk from here, as the inn grounds are leased from the estate. It's a lovely old place—Tudor, mostly, and filled with eighteenth-century furniture."

"Solid?"

"Still solid. There isn't a chair you can't sit on and stay so. But I give you the pathway you have to walk along from the inn to get to it. It meanders through a grove of cypress trees all of which have their feet planted in chocolate-colored water and their branches dripping with Spanish moss. Honestly, they look famished to the point of starvation for a good stomach-filling murder."

"I will ask you to remember, Margot, that homicide is one form of service which we do not supply—puritanical though the attitude may be."

"I will, Jake. Good night."

The lane returning from the inn to the Tyler cottage wound between banks of fragrant shrubs that were silvered and blackly shadowed by the moon. Paths branched off at intervals to the cottages of the other Wynstable guests. Even though the hour was just after ten, it seemed, from the cemetery stillness, from the absence of lights in windows, that all of them had convalescently gone to bed.

Margot breathed deeply of the night, feeling comfortably tired herself and quite willing to turn in. As she neared the cottage occupied by the Millays a darker shadow against a dark clump of palmettos became pinpointed by the glowing tip of a cigar. It would be the adonic Forrest with his pulverizing looks and accomplished charm, and he must have been aware of her walking past, but he did not speak.

Turning in toward the Tyler cottage, with her footsteps muffled on the pathway's sand, Margot heard low voices. One of them she recognized as Francine's. She hesitated at intruding, especially so when she realized that Francine and her companion were deliberately hurting each other in fierce, sad whispers, but the thought of Forrest Millay's motionless figure darkly pressed among the palmettos gave her an uncomfortable sense of threat.

She called softly: "Hello—Francine?"

Rounding a mass of hibiscus, she saw Francine clearly in the strong moonlight. The girl's face was set hard in a furious anger, and her hair was disheveled as though strong fingers had been shoved into it. Her lipstick job was a squashed mess. A man's back confronted Margot. It was a big back, broad-shouldered under taut white linen, and it looked muscle-bunched and set.

"Oh—you," Francine said. She jammed her hair back into some sort of shape, which still did not prevent it from resembling the fright wig that had been worn so tellingly by Medusa. "This self-styled cavalier is Bruce Calverse, Miss Gilland. You will find him the very flower of chivalry at its Southern best."

So far as the flower part went Margot wouldn't know, but she did find her hand being enveloped in a portable crushing machine while hot, bewildered, hurt eyes in a young face of dark granite glowered down at her.

"I know why Mrs. Tyler asked you to come here, Miss Gilland. Can you possibly beat some sense into this tantrum-ridden nitwit?"

"You seem to have been making a pretty good go at it yourself, Mr. Calverse—that is, if a near scalping rates par for the course."

This light approach landed with a thud. But it did restore a touch of balance to Bruce's aplomb, for he smothered the outward effects of his seething, wished both Francine and Margot a bitterly formal good night, and, in the stately manner of a Sherman tank, left them flat.

Margot said in a quiet voice to Francine: "I think you ought to know that Forrest Millay in all probability was an interested observer of your main bout."

Francine's eyes lost their anger. Her face looked very young, and it was twisted briefly with a wrench of downright fear.

"I remember it now. I remember smelling cigar smoke. Thank you, Miss Gilland."

"Would you—won't you please let me help you if I can?" For an instant Margot believed that the girl was about to break, about to share whatever it was that was torturing her so. For it was some form of torture, there was no doubt about that. But she did not.

"You can help me best by leaving me alone, strictly alone. I mean that. I swear that if you try to butt in I'll do something to prevent it. Something pretty final, Miss Gilland."

Francine ran, then, almost stumblingly toward the cottage door. Margot waited to let her get inside. Melissa, she thought, was right. Francine still was desperately in love with Bruce Calverse. The act she was putting on with Forrest Millay was all wrong. It was as phony as a big, paste stone. It was as dangerous as the gun you didn't think was loaded.

CHAPTER 5

On the following morning, Saturday, June fifth, Mrs. Frosher experienced such a flood of relief over the departure of the Tylers for Brandgwyn that her guards were down. She felt that the exodus had resulted in an instant revivification of the Wynstable's social impeccability. In fact, she felt almost mellow, an emotion so radically unfamiliar that it contributed in a large measure to her acceptance of Cloquette.

Any thought of animal pets being harbored at the Wynstable was simply absurd. The circumstances, however, were extreme, including the unheard-of mellowing. They involved an Atlanta spinster, a Miss Amnessa Lynndecourt whose blood was so deeply blue that it flirted with a royal purple.

Miss Lynndecourt proposed to convalesce for several weeks from a mild attack of the influenza, which was all right. With her would be her companion, a Miss Mabel Tishman. This in turn was all to the good, inasmuch as Miss Tishman's blood was of a sufficient, if watery, blue. It fell somewhere in the spectrum near to the shade known as Alice.

But also with Miss Lynndecourt, and as inseparable from her existence as a left arm or leg, was Cloquette. This wasn't so hot.

Cloquette was a flaccid, insufferably unattractive pug bitch whose face presented all the unadmirable features of a freighter whose bows had been caved in by a collision. In addition to this silent drawback the beast was afflicted with an unappetizing, wheezing snuffle. Fatly, she weighed her breed's maximum of eighteen pounds, and her short coat favored the apricot-fawn variation in color. Age had toned this to the tint of prepared mustard. Miss Lynndecourt, uniquely, loved her.

To house this horror in the inn proper was naturally out of the question, but Mrs. Frosher did turn over to Miss Lynndecourt the cottage that had just been vacated by the Tylers. A touch of spite entered into this. It lay in the cottage's adjacency to the one occupied by the Millays.

The jilting of Bruce Calverse by Francine and her pyrotechnically developed interest in Forrest Millay had seeped like a corrosive acid through the county's better blood streams. They had nothing against the Millays, but they had nothing for them, either: regarding them merely as reasonably well-surfaced outsiders from the dam-yankee hinterland and, as such, acceptable objects for financially profitable toleration.

But a Calverse jilted had altered all of that. It had focused on the Millays a shaft of outrage which was as intense as the one beamed at Francine.

A good deal of this, in the most petty manner, had motivated Mrs. Frosher's willingness to permit Cloquette a next-door residence, no matter how repulsively her snuffling wheezes might react upon the (now) leprous Millays.

The sting of this minor spite was considerably blunted when, upon being introduced, Penelope Millay said to Miss Lynndecourt: "I also had a pug when I was young. I just about cried my heart out when she died."

"Distemper, Mrs. Millay?"

"No, Miss Lynndecourt. A fishbone. Papa had been sent a salmon from the Gaspe."

This, too, was of importance.

CHAPTER 6

The settling-in process at Brandgwyn was accomplished with that ease which great wealth so smoothly can effect. Miss Brandgwyn's staff had remained in service at Melissa's request.

They had also stayed on from a curiosity so compelling that not one of them, down to the last stable boy, could have been blasted from his job—the curiosity revolving around the scenographic Mr. Tyler, his whizzing knives, and the delicious possibilities ever latent in a state of social ostracism. They were effectively operative, in a deceptively retarded fashion, under the ancient eye of Jarvis. Jarvis was the Paleozoic major-domo of the plantation.

Margot was assigned an upstairs suite in the south wing. She adapted its sitting room into a semi-office for the handling of mail which still pelted Melissa, although by now in an ebbing volume. It took her the morning and most of the afternoon to make a dent in the letters that had accumulated during Melissa's run up to New York.

She disposed tactfully of fourteen inventions, declining the opportunity for investing a varying scale of thousands toward furthering their development, although one—a device for making musical balloons—did hold her wavering in an Elsa Maxwell state of vivid fascination.

She firmly rejected an assortment of priceless invitations to sink large sums in dazzling real-estate ventures, gold mines, oil wells, and secretly discovered deposits of uranium. She also turned down cold a couple of compelling offers from California mediums to unveil the future—one by means of a standardized crystal ball and the other being more intriguingly based on emanations from a genuine finger bone, filched at fantastic cost from the tomb of Merlin the Great.

Three out of twenty-seven appeals both for personal and public charity were set aside for Melissa's later consideration. Then she came to a cold, shocked pause at one letter that had been canceled at the Charleston post office several days ago. It was signed simply: An Earnest Friend.

It read:

My Dear Mrs. Tyler,

When considering your daughter's coming recital in benefit of the Cecil Willisman House restoration may I suggest, for your additional consideration, the fact that our County Clerk was a classmate of Mr. Bruce Calverse at the Academy and that it is their pleasure, on occasion, to go mullet fishing together?

An Earnest Friend

That was all there was to it, and yet its content of a single sentence sent a warning douche of ice down Margot's back.

To her way of thinking, the note expanded out to this: some transaction of record had come to the county clerk's attention in his official capacity. Its existence presumably would be relayed to Bruce Calverse during one of their friendly excursions after mullets. With, inferentially, a waspish assortment of painful results.

In some fashion the matter obviously touched on Francine's interests. It would practically have to, to be of any strong interest to the jilted Bruce. Just as presumably, it therefore could touch Forrest Millay's interests as well.

A marriage license?

Had that been the basis for the free-for-all between Bruce and Francine last night, at which Forrest had been such a definitely non-cheering spectator?

Or did it indicate a time element?

Was its deadline the recital, billed for next Saturday? The note distinctly spoke of it for consideration. Was something more drastic than song to be slated for its program?

Margot put the letter among her personal papers in the desk. Her job at Brandgwyn was largely to act as a shield between just such eventualities and the Tylers. She determined on an investigation along two lines before disturbing Melissa. A discreet descent on the county clerk's office was an obvious one. Jake, from New York, would have to arrange that some reliable contact in Charleston handle it.

The other, the more difficult line, was Mrs. Calverse. She had originated the recital, with its now possibly dangerous time element of next Saturday. And there was the additional peculiar fact that her sponsorship of Francine still remained so remarkably unshaken. An opportunity for exploring this came with almost coincidental suddenness.

Melissa had driven with Henry into Charleston, both for some shopping and to pick up Francine at Signor Castelaronni's studio. Shortly before five o'clock Jarvis came to Margot and said that Mrs. Braintree Calverse was downstairs in the green drawing room. Mrs. Calverse had expressed a desire to converse with Miss Gilland while awaiting Mrs.

Tyler's return from town, if Miss Gilland was not otherwise occupied and if she would be so kind.

Brandgwyn's green drawing room was an impressive job, being beautifully detailed in its woodwork and in the plaster carvings of its ceiling. The glittering cascades of a crystal chandelier hung from the ceiling's center. It had never been electrified, and it drove the servants, after each usage of its candles, into fits.

The room's wallpaper was in the Chinese motif so stereotypically fashionable for the period, and gloomy as sin. Its spotting of venerable furniture notably included an early spinet (not converted into a desk) and a gaming table at which Jerome Bonaparte, when *en tour* about the United States, was allegedly reputed to have lost his cambric shirt.

Mrs. Calverse sat against the rich red brocade of a Sheraton sofa. Her white gloved hands were restful over a needle-point bag on her lap, and her diminutive shoes were decorously formalized upon the room's large Aubusson carpet. A froth of pale velvet violets remotely indicated themselves as a hat. She looked as appealingly harmless as a vanilla meringue glace.

This was a deadly mistake. Her grandfather had been the historically respected General Alfred Eustace (Old Lobster Claw) Bellinghue. He had soundly grounded Mrs. Calverse during her childhood in those shell-crunching, pincer-jawed, tactical strategies which had won him his crustacean nickname on the battlefield.

As Margot came into the room both she and Mrs. Calverse exchanged one penetrating look of mutual evaluation. Each woman was brilliantly deceived.

Margot saw the charming prototype of a Southern gentlewoman at her sheltered best. This was perfectly true, of course, but it did not dig deeply enough.

Mrs. Calverse saw an attractive young woman who unobtrusively wore the insignia of good breeding and assured position. She failed, however, to assess the cold precision of intelligence masked behind Margot's simple white pique front—an omission for which Old Lobster Claw would have dressed her down strappingly.

Anne Calverse had two voices, one for her various club activities and the other being what some carpers called her Little Eva. The latter was soft and low. It suggested those overtones of feminine helplessness which generations of Southern belles had developed into a fine art. She used it now.

"So awfully good of you, Miss Gilland. I just know you must be busy as a bee."

She had come, she said, for a definite decision from Francine about the program. What with the recital being only a week away, the printer, not unreasonably, demanded it. So far the list had been in flux—some French and Italian arias, some lieder, and a few spirituals.

Mrs. Calverse moved a step further. She planted the points that Bruce had spoken of having met Miss Gilland last night and that Bruce (this, evidently, as a carte-blanche dispensation for his fire-eating routines) was such a romantic, such a hotheaded dear primarily because he took after his father, dear Braintree, who perpetually teetered on the brink of palsy over some bother or other.

Then at last Mrs. Calverse got down to business.

"Melissa has told me about all the clever and even real personal matters which Mr. Harden's office manages to handle, Miss Gilland."

"Yes, we do take a stab at almost anything, Mrs. Calverse."

"Well, I declare, it almost seems to me to imply omniscience. That's why I doubt whether my little piece of news isn't already known to you—I mean about that good-looking young Mr. Forrest Millay and Francine? About their having made plans to elope?"

Margot, after a slight trip, succeeded in taking this in her stride.

"Are you certain of this, Mrs. Calverse?"

"Yes indeed. They're planning to fly to some Gretna Green or other up in Maryland on next Saturday night, right after the recital."

Awareness of such things, Mrs. Calverse explained, was simple when you understood the infinite tentacles of the grapevine among plantation servants. A gesture symbolically dotted each twig, each keyhole, with a glued-on ear.

"It's the reason why I wanted to talk with you, Miss Gilland, before Melissa got back."

Margot still felt the setup to be cloudily devious, even after Mrs. Calverse added that she had thought they ought to consult. One reaction did come on the oblique: if Francine and Forrest were flying to Maryland for a short-order wedding, then the news which An Earnest Friend so darkly had hinted at as lying in the county clerk's office would scarcely be a marriage license. That could become operative only right here in South Carolina.

"Consult in what way, Mrs. Calverse?"

"About telling Melissa."

There was a stiff etiquette to the grapevine, Mrs. Calverse explained. Its tidbits might properly be hinted at (stark-nakedly) to any number of mistresses—who in turn must politely pretend to be stone-deaf—but they must never be whispered directly to the principals involved, in this instance the Tylers.

"And that's why I feel just positive that neither Melissa nor Mr. Tyler knows anything about the elopement, Miss Gilland."

The situation was much clearer to Margot now. Mrs. Calverse wanted the elopement spiked. For her son's sake. Apparently she had strongly approved of what had started out so clinchingly to be a match between him and Francine. And she still held hopes that the monkey wrench, represented by Forrest Millay, would be removed. It would explain her continued sponsoring of Francine after the jilting. But this hope would be irretrievably killed if the elopement were to go through.

"I agree with you that Mrs. Tyler will have to know, Mrs. Calverse. I suppose—what you really wish is that I should tell her, isn't it?"

For a moment the Little Eva guard was down and Mrs. Calverse looked both her true strength and her age. It was a battle strength, and one which would blast into ruin any opposition which stood in the path of her objective.

"Yes, Miss Gilland, that is it. I'm sure you will understand that in view of how my son and Francine once felt about one another how cruelly embarrassing it would be to tell Melissa myself."

* * * *

Later, in the evening when dinner was over, Margot asked Melissa to join her in her sitting room. She spoke of the elopement rumor and of its source, and as she talked a heavy apathy settled on Melissa, one which seemed deadening both to her muscles and her mind.

"I don't know what to say, Miss Gilland. I simply don't. Can you understand how I feel? Why I wouldn't have the right to influence Francine one way or the other?"

"I can't exactly, Mrs. Tyler."

"It's because of Henry. Henry and me."

In a fashion, Melissa said, it was a repeat of their own pattern. She had been nineteen, just as Francine now was, when she had decamped with Henry—not in an Eastern Air Lines crack job, but in one of the Drury Shows carnival trucks. She was trying terribly hard to be fair because she remembered so clearly how she had felt in that long-ago day.

"I'm thinking what I would have missed if they had caught or forcibly stopped me. Or if they had found out and had argued me out of it. Or if I'd lacked the courage. It's life I'd have missed, Miss Gilland. Just all of my life."

"But on the plane, Mrs. Tyler, you told me you felt that Francine still was in love with Bruce Calverse."

"Yes, I've thought of that, and I still do. But that doesn't mean she is. You're closer to nineteen than I am. It's easier for you to think back.

Were you always sure how you felt about people? Weren't there swift intensities and then just as swift a change?"

Margot mentally retreated several years and realized that what Melissa had said was true. She dusted off Harry, a lifeguard at Easthampton's Leach. For several weeks he had had her in a blister which she had felt sure was the real thing. Until he had broken out his consuming passion for practical jokes. An effect known as the squirting boutonniere was the number that had got her.

Harry's successor had been a stupefyingly handsome character christened Wilbur Longtwine, whose father had owned a bank. Wilbur positively had been it. He had been it for a full two months until an ash blonde named Doris amiably had let Margot in on the news that a Wilbur Junior or a Wilburess was due to increase the population come October.

Margot kept the lid clamped tight on Johnny. On Tarawa. On the telegram. She had been older then. About as old as she had felt she could ever get.

"Of course you're completely right, Mrs. Tyler. But tell me this—would you object to a marriage between Forrest and Francine?"

"No. I shall always feel she is free to marry anyone she cares to."

"Does she know this?"

"I'm sure she must."

"Then it's hard to understand the elopement angle, unless it's a romantic gesture. I can't quite see Francine going in for romantic gestures."

"She wouldn't. She detests them." Melissa looked thoroughly wretched. "Miss Gilland, for the time being, I think, we will just let the matter rest."

CHAPTER 7

Midnight struck and the date became Sunday, June sixth.

In the hush of the house, after the Tylers had retired, Margot went downstairs to a room just off the library where Cousin Elizabeth had cooked up her varied and lucrative business affairs. It contained Brandgwyn's single telephone.

She called Jake in New York and told him about the rumored elopement, and its unreasonableness.

"It worries me," she said. "I'd almost swear that Francine is being jostled into it against her will by Forrest Millay. The charming rat."

"Rat, nonsense. He's a sterling character."

The Cleveland branch, Jake said, had put Davis right on the job, and Davis's preliminary spadework had left the Millays with an excellent record. Naturally, further diggings might change it.

The Wade Park Manor, where they kept an expensive suite on a year-round basis, was pleased with them. They had been resident now for two years, using it largely as a *pied-à-terre* to return to from their trips. They traveled a great deal.

Locally they had few visitors, and only rarely entertained. It was considered that the effects of Mrs. Millay's illness had made her guest-shy—the rental clerk vaguely recalled her having specified it as something which sounded like delayed progeria. He thought that Mrs. Millay must have considered it a little ridiculous because of the quality of her smile.

"Anyhow, Margot, they kept very much to themselves, whatever the reason. It sounds like the usual threadbare mother complex to me."

"No, Jake. Remember I've met him. The only silver cord that could anchor that comely Gila monster would be his mother's strangle clutch on the purse strings."

Jake went into Forrest's war record, which was, he said, just one of those things. Stavely, in the Washington agency, had dug out a few items of indifferent sorts. Nothing discreditable, but nothing on the creditable side, either.

Stavely had caught the impression that political pressure had been used to seat Forrest right there in the Pentagon for the duration.

Harmlessly, and certainly safely so far as his handsome hide was concerned. The source of the political pressure was unnamed, beyond the slenderest hint that it involved the head of a powerful state machine.

About the only derogatory comment which Stavely's Navy source definitely had made was a crack that Forrest had shown no signs of any unbearable eagerness to get his lovely hulk transferred into some form of combat duty. He had clung tenaciously to his swivel chair like a true-blue limpet.

"That's all we know up to now, Margot, except that Mrs. Millay does hold the purse strings and her drawing account is solid. It's too soon to have heard from Jaffries in Los Angeles, hut I'll call you when his report comes in."

"There's one other thing that has come up," Margot said.

She explained the letter signed An Earnest Friend and asked Jake to get in touch with some Charleston lawyer who would not be suspected of having any interest in the Tylers, the Calverses, or the Millays. She wanted him to find out what, if anything, had been recorded in the county clerk's office during the week before last that would touch on any of the three families.

"I'll see to it," Jake said. "Today is Sunday, so you won't be hearing from whoever handles it before Monday."

They said good night.

Thin moonlight sifted into the library through a bank of french doors, and Margot saw that one door was standing ajar. She did not remember it having been so when she had gone through the room just before.

She stood at it for a while looking out across the moon-bright pattern toward the south. It covered a great stretch of lawn which ran to the steel geometrics of a formal garden and, still further beyond, to the start of the cypress grove, the clear silhouette of which was so greyly muted under what well could have been the tatters of the dead.

She thought it must have been the night's scented breeze that had nudged the french door ajar. Then an alien odor on the flowery air impressed her with a touch of shock. It was simple to identify once she had concentrated on it. Faintly but unmistakably it overrode the jasmine fragrance: the odor of a cigar.

It punctuated the day's general sense of unease. It linked with the shadowy Forrest, so still last night against the palmettos. It increased the quality of furtiveness which Margot felt about him. A blood-cooling word, furtiveness. With it inseparability from intents that were tricky, and dangerous, and evil.

The incident did not go toward furthering a good night's rest.

CHAPTER 8

Brilliant morning sunlight did a good deal toward erasing the nervous thoughts of night, and the balance of that Sunday offered little of direct importance.

Forrest walked over from the Wynstable after breakfast with the decorous intention of escorting Francine and Melissa to church: a *beau geste* that had been established during the Tylers' stay at the inn. His getup and manner could not have been more churchlike.

Margot would have given a lot to ask him just what he had been up to with his cigar-smoking midnight prowling and ajar-french-doors, and her hackles rose at his perfect characterization of a wholesome, upstanding young American male embarked with his best girl and her mother toward their devotions.

Henry, who had a solid respect for religion in what best could be called a laissez-faire sense, did not join them. Nor did Margot. It had struck her that the opportunity was excellent for a casual call on Mrs. Millay, whose convalescing prescribed as little physical movement as possible. She wanted to open the tap through which all mothers gushed about their sons. She wanted every drop of low-down on Forrest that she could get: even a maternally biased one.

Her excuse for this minor fishing trip would be that she thought she might have left a scarf—compact—anything—when moving from the Tyler cottage, and had walked over to ask about it. This done, then the thoughtful call on the solitary Mrs. Millay.

It was very simple. Margot evaded the inn proper, and hence Mrs. Frosher, who would have cornered her and gone in for some fishing on her own hook. She went directly to the cottage, where she found that its new occupants, Miss Lynndecourt and Miss Tishman, also were off to church. They had deposited Cloquette in an inert, suety blob on Mrs. Millay's neighboring patio under her kindly eye. Margot went over and explained.

"I'm always leaving something or other behind too, Miss Gilland. Forrest says it's the subconscious expression of a wash to return. He's so terribly clever about psychological things. Do sit down. I believe the services wall be over soon."

Margot took an armchair beside Mrs. Millay s bamboo chaise longue. The sun was almost over-generously health-giving, but Mrs. Millay seemed to love it.

"I'll just wait a moment," Margot said, "because the scarf is completely unimportant. I came over for the walk, really."

It was an agreeable quarter of an hour, the talk being channeled with ease by Margot into Forrest. Mrs. Millay's expected eulogies flowed forth even to the point of being illustrated, if not exactly with colored slides at least with photographs.

Margot respectfully viewed the handsome Forrest as a boy in an Eton jacket, as a smaller boy in a sailor suit, and finally (backed up against the limit) as a garbless baby in arms, with his mother's head bent down in a dizzy look of glutted admiration.

With the pageant over, Margot's only helpful reaction to it lay in the pictures' backgrounds. They all had the estate look, the indefinable stamp of accustomed wealth and established family roots. To a measure this was good, but she knew how fairly commonplace it was for a good, solid family in the upper brackets to produce either a dud or an exceedingly shady black sheep.

She went in for a delicate sortie toward finding out whether or not Mrs. Millay knew of the proposed elopement. The approaches which she used were light and of the sort so easily swallowable by a doting mother. How much it must mean to Mrs. Millay to have the companionship of such a devoted son. What a pity that with time one's children left the nest and carved an existence of their own—that sort of thing, but laid on with a spatula rather than a trowel.

Mrs. Millay's smile was fatuously assured.

"I doubt whether Forrest ever will, Miss Gilland. A normal, a companionable interest in girls, yes. But he's not the type for marriage. Frankly, he's too self-centered."

Walking back to Brandgwyn, Margot realized that the eulogies, so far as much concrete data went, had produced actually nothing. Then she wondered whether in a negative way they hadn't. Whether their very generalities had not been purposely thrown up as a shield between the portrait of a son as Mrs. Millay wished people to accept Forrest and, perhaps, a far grimmer portrait of Forrest as he truly was.

She did carry away one strange souvenir of the call: without any specific definition of why she did so, she felt sorry for Mrs. Millay.

The hours moved on with their soporific lack of entanglements. During the afternoon Margot did some work on Melissa's mail, and even it produced no startling plums to give the enveloping lethargy a jolt.

At dinner she was introduced via Angelica, the Brandgwyn Cordon Bleu, to oyster crabs in sherry, and to gopher stew—a regional gourmet's delight, the main substance of which translated itself into the meat of jaywalking land tortoises.

Toward twelve she went to bed and slept.

CHAPTER 9

Monday, June seventh's opening gun was a call from Jake which came through shortly after lunch.

"I've heard from Los Angeles," Jake said, "and it's just possible that Jaffries may have run onto a lead."

They could forget the crank and threatening-letter stuff, or at any rate it could be put on ice. Jaffries was satisfied there was nothing more to it than the district attorney or the postal people had thought.

The former Tyler home and its neighbors also seemed to have offered nothing which could be considered helpful. They remembered the Tylers quite vividly, but only from the sudden-inheritance angle, the pot-of-gold stuff at the rainbow's end. Henry's knife hurling, at which he kept, in practice in the back yard, was ignored with Hollywoodian indifference, and his tattooing left them blasé. It would have had to have been done in luminous paint to warrant even a second look.

When blandished by Jaffries in her studio on La Brea, Francine's voice teacher had been a bit better. Evidently Madame Destina Vesturi was a volatile piece, always in full cry, and with the emotional balance of an uninhibited blast furnace. She had shredded Francine to the core, lauding her as a girl of utmost fascination and vocal promise and so rich! So how you say? So stinkpot rich! A type. Men? No. Many noes. No men.

Her frothing had simmered down to a single useful drop which Jaffries had latched onto. Francine was devastatingly but nuts about swimming and the ocean. She used to hotfoot it out to Hermosa Beach every chance she got, usually with another pupil—female—who owned a car.

Jaffries had looked the pupil up: a Janice Heather. In a nutshell, Miss Heather had a Hermosa Beach boy friend named Jimmy Smith with whom she would sun-bathe on the golden, oil-flecked sand while Francine got kicked around by the breakers.

"By the way, Margot, did you know that Francine was tattooed?"

"Oh no, Jake! Not—extensively?"

"No, just a small token gesture of defiance. A little bust of George Washington on her left thigh. It's visible when she wears a swim suit. As what isn't."

Miss Heather had told Jaffries that Francine had had the tattoo done to confute the queasy critics of her father's more wholesale job, as an open declaration that she was on his side and she loved him. Sort of childish, Jaffries had thought, but nice.

"Now here is the lead, Margot."

Shortly after the blaze of publicity had broken about the Tylers having inherited the bumper Brandgwyn fortune, Miss Heathers Jimmy had divulged that a pal of his would like to meet Francine.

"That sounds too crude for it to have been Forrest, Jake."

"It was crude, but according to Jaffries, Jimmy is not exactly a polished devotee of the subtle. Nor could have been his pal."

"Well, then, wasn't it just an ordinary fortune hunter or a common garden wolf?"

"Jaffries doesn't think so."

It seemed that before the rendezvous could be arranged some illiterate California weather had knocked Janice Heather flat with the flu. By the time she had recovered, the Tylers had left for Parnellton and—this was what had interested Jaffries—Jimmy Smith had buttoned up. He had refused to tell Miss Heather who his pal was, or whether Francine actually had or had not met him. On the other hand, he did tell Miss Headier, in what she had considered a chilly tone of voice, to forget it.

Point two: Jimmy's job had been that of a perambulating photographer, largely among the bathers on the beach. It was how he had met Miss Heather.

"There could be a link in that, Jake—Forrest's interest in photography."

"Could be."

Jimmy's income from his work could scarcely have leveled much higher than the hot-dog stage, and yet, when Jaffries located him, he had found Jimmy to be the affluently dressed owner of a newly opened, first-rate portrait studio on the Strip.

"Blackmail?"

"Either that or extortion, Margot. It certainly wasn't the result of any overwhelming genius."

In addition to having buttoned up on Miss Heather, Jimmy had icily refused to have any truck with Jaffries. Money as an inducement had been looked upon thoughtfully but coldly. Jaffries thought, however, that with time and by boosting the ante he eventually would get him. But right now Jimmy boy was what Jaffries described as a badly aghast young man.

"Jake, there just *isn't* time. If that elopement is to be stopped, I've got to have something concrete to spike it with before Saturday night."

"Well, that gives him five days, Margot. Don't worry about it. Jaffries is good."

About an hour after this telephone call Melissa said to Margot: "I wonder whether you would please help us, Miss Gilland? Francine and I are trying to decide which dress would be best for the recital."

They gathered upstairs in Melissa's sitting room. It was a strange modeling. Francine had consciously avoided any contact with Margot, except at mealtimes, but she could not do so now. Because of her mother's presence, there was no open show of antagonism, but her manner held an acrid tinge, like the after-smell of wetted smoke.

Melissa, too, was heartfully trying to act as if everything were normal, as if she were ignorant of the fact that whichever dress was chosen for the concert platform would also serve, at least at the start, for the elopement flight into heaven knew what sort of a future with Forrest.

Such smiling as was done was very set. There were three dresses to choose from, all of them high style, and two were Paris originals.

"They're good, they're beautiful," Margot said, "but for this specific appearance—I mean we must realize it will be a personal debut in a sense, rather than simply a recital. To put it bluntly, the audience will be critical of the singing, but they will be doubly critical of Francine herself. If it makes any sense, these dresses are *too* good, too stamped with a knowing perfection."

"Miss Gilland," Melissa said, "that's what I felt, too, only I couldn't express it. If you will excuse me for a moment?"

Melissa went into her dressing room, leaving Margot and Francine in a suspended state of cold, artificial silence. She returned carrying a dress.

"Will you try this, dear? Cousin Elizabeth gave it to me for my nineteenth birthday. I left with your father before the ball for which it was meant."

It was a beautiful gown of dairy-gold satin brocaded in bands, fragile, deceptively simple, and, while giving an impression of the bare, actually it was not.

"Yes," Margot said, "that's it."

At five o'clock in the afternoon Jarvis rapped on Margot's living-room door. There was, he said, a Mr. Frankworth Ranger calling on the telephone. She went downstairs. The voice on the wire was courteous, impartially efficient.

"I've looked up that matter which Mr. Harden phoned me about, Miss Gilland."

"Oh yes, Mr. Ranger?"

"On June first a marriage license was issued in the names of Mr. Forrest Millay and Miss Francine Tyler. There are no further records which bear on the inquiry. However—"

"Yes?"

"You will accept this, please, as nothing but an unconfirmed rumor? You will estimate it accordingly? It concerns the third family required in my report. The word is going around in certain quarters of the city that Mr. Braintree Calverse's financial condition is dangerously close to the point of collapse. May I express a purely personal conviction in regard to this?"

"I wish that you would."

"I do not believe that either Mrs. Calverse or Bruce Calverse are in any sense aware of Mr. Calverse's precarious state. And that is all, Miss Gilland. If I can be of any later service to you, please let me know."

"Thank you, Mr. Ranger. I will."

Margot remained seated at the telephone after she had hung up. So it *had* been a marriage license after all. The answer to what must have occurred after its issuance on June first to have had its use discarded was surely a repellent one. Deplorable enough to have the ceremony, to which Melissa would have raised no objections, replaced with the furtive design of swift and secret flight to some distant justice of the peace in Maryland.

An Earnest Friend.

Certainly Mrs. Calverse hadn't written the anonymous letter, for of her own accord she had brought the elopement plan out into the open. But was this true? Had her anonymity been an early stab to expose the marriage license and had she then discarded it when faced with the need of direct action because of the nearness of Saturday night?

One other thing made sense to her puzzling continuance in sponsoring Francine. In spite of Ranger's belief that Mrs. Calverse was ignorant of her husband's collapsing fortune, it was quite possible that she was perfectly aware of it. If this were true, then her maneuvers would not solely be directed toward patching Bruce's broken heart. They would in addition be directed toward patching the Calverse moneybags through a wedding with Melissa's wealth.

An Earnest Friend. The phrase continued its nagging. *If* not Mrs. Calverse, who then?

Why?

CHAPTER 10

Tuesday, June eighth, opened agreeably with Margot's wardrobe luggage reaching Brandgwyn by express from New York. The morning further was punctuated with the delivery of two Cadillacs which Melissa had ordered as surprise gifts for Francine and Henry. Both were convertibles, Francine's being a canary yellow and Henry's a stratosphere blue. They were knockouts.

"It was to have been such a happy surprise, Miss Gilland," Melissa said while Francine and Henry were outside on the driveway looking the cars over. "But now, as things are, it just isn't very happy. Is it that way with money?"

"Sometimes. It won't have to be so with you, Mrs. Tyler. Things will straighten out."

"I like clichés, Miss Gilland. They're comforting when you're in trouble. Like it's always darkest just before the dawn, and the cloud with the silver lining. I like them because sometimes they turn out to be true."

The manner in which Henry and Francine reacted to the cars was throat-catching. They crushed Melissa with hugging her and telling her how happy she had made them. They weren't, of course, but the performance was thoroughly convincing as an expression of the love each felt for her. Henry caught Melissa up bodily. He put her in the stratosphere blue to take her for the first ride, shouting to Francine to follow with Margot in the canary yellow.

Francine didn't follow. Instead she took the road to Parnellton, which was scarcely over a mile south of the plantation. She drove like an automaton, with her grip on the wheel unnecessarily hard, and Margot's few tentative breaks into conversational comments were met with a sullen silence. She pulled up at the curb before Lingworth's drugstore on Jerrybone Street, which was in the center of the town's shopping district.

"I have to telephone," she said. "Come in, Miss Gilland, if you care to look around."

Margot followed Francine across the tree-shaded sidewalk and they entered the drugstore's large, dim interior. Francine went directly to a telephone booth in the rear and shut herself in.

It was a moment before Margot's eyes could adjust themselves from the strong outdoor blaze of sun to the room's comparative twilight. The back of a man seated over at the soda fountain came into focus, then into familiarity as being Bruce Calverse's. The back looked just as muscle-bunched and set as it had by the hibiscus clump last Friday night.

Bruce seemed unaware of Margot where she stood partly masked by a magazine rack, and equally unaware that his sparring partner of the other evening had passed behind him and vanished into the telephone booth. Moodily wrapped in a dark, private trance, he went on with drinking a coke.

The only other human visible in the store was the counterman: a towheaded youngster with Southern, dreamy eyes, who limply leaned in a saturation of inertia against the service shelf along the wall. Such, in its pallid, tableaued hush, were the setting and the cast when, with a breezy slam of the street door, Forrest Millay came in.

"Did those film packs get here yet?" he said with a busy directness to the counterman.

"No, sir. We are still expecting."

From her box-seat view at the magazine rack Margot noticed Bruce's back stiffen and the deliberation with which he lowered the glass of coke and freed his fingers from it. She then saw Forrest grow aware of Bruce.

"Bruce Calverse, isn't it?" Forrest said. He held out his hand. "Francine's spoken of you. I'm Millay."

Bruce stood up. It had the effect of a lengthening rather than of standing. He ignored Forrest's hand. He placed a dime on the counter and said: "Here's for the coke, Larry."

"Thanks, Bruce. Be seeing you."

"Sure will."

Forrest's hand gave up its mid-air, silly look of ostracism and moved sideways to rest on the counter. Under its tan his face whitened with a swift, uncontrollable surge of rage.

"Well, I guess it's true," he said. "That the South and its people have always been bad losers."

The counterman clicked the empty coke glass he was rinsing against metal. A fly droned with witlessly important swoops above the syrup taps. Time ceased.

"My car's outside, Mr. Millay," Bruce said. "Will you drive with me, sir, to some place that's less public?"

"Oh, ship it, Calverse. You sound like a Class Z horse opera."

Bruce's fist seemed scarcely to move in its transit, to explode against Forrest's face. The bout was short-lived, and the incidental, innocent-bystander damage wasn't heavy—a table display of bathing caps, dark glasses, suntan lotions—a flying migration of personalized greeting cards—but for the headliners it was pretty bloody. Neither came out the clear winner, or rather both did, whichever way you cared to look at it. Their breathing was deep and painful after they stopped.

"Mr. Millay, I'm going to kill you if you don't go away from us," Bruce said.

* * * *

The most puzzling aftermath of this meeting of fists was, for Margot, the fact that on the following morning (Wednesday, June ninth) Francine, with Forrest beside her, went in for what amounted to a slow, public parade in the yellow convertible through the streets of Parnellton.

She chose the shopping hour when the chain stores were at their housewifely busiest. Her expression was considered by the many who saw it as being animatedly lively. Forrest's expression was less easily determined, due to a taped-up busted nose and a black eye.

The only reason for the exhibition that Margot could dope out was that Forrest had forced it as an open avowal that Francine was for him, that he had compelled the cheap spectacle through the strength of whatever the hold was which he held over the girl. For it was no longer possible not to believe that there was some such hold.

Melissa knew about the parade and about yesterday's sickening fight. She was increasingly shaky as the day progressed, and inclined to become uncertain in her physical movements—such as upsetting a water glass at the dining table, bumping against objects of furniture, such things.

"I wish we could just call off the recital, Miss Gilland," she said, when alone for a moment with Margot after dinner "Almost I wish we had never come to Brandgwyn at all."

Henry said no about canceling the recital, when Melissa mentioned it to him later. It would be a cowardly thing to do, he thought, and he was sure that Melissa would think it over and agree.

Shortly before she turned in that night, Margot had a telephone call from Jake. It concerned Davis's deeper delvings into the Cleveland past of the Millays. One of their rare dinner guests at the Wade Park Manor had been remembered and identified by an elevator operator.

The guest's name was Pittcairn. Until immediately after the war, when a reform revolt had thrown both him and his corrupt political machine out of power, he had for years held an apparently unbreakable strangle hold over a Midwestern state.

"Forrest strikes me as being too much on the weak-sister side," Margot said, "to have been of much value to any organization of that importance."

"Davis isn't so sure. He's going on with it even though the machine is beaten and Pittcairn possibly nothing more to the Millays than a onetime dinner guest. He is taking a morning flight for Pittcairn's home town."

There had been no further report from Jaffries on the Los Angeles, Jimmy Smith end.

The next day, Thursday, June tenth, was marked for Margot by a single incident which carried her concern pretty close to the edge of fear. There was no tangible reason why it should have, for it held no melodramatics in the accepted sense of such things, and yet it did the trick. And it did it, furthermore, entirely in pantomime.

The moon was two nights short of the full, and the lawn below the opened windows of her bedroom resembled a disk of burnished silver. She was about to retire and was standing for a moment in the darkness looking out.

She saw Francine and Henry walking across the lawn toward the house. Neither was speaking. Then, in this wordlessness, when they were close and most clearly within Margot's vision, they stood face to face.

Francine swayed.

She flung herself against her father in an abandonment of despair, while he too seemed to cling to her with a strong fury of protection. Her sobbing was of the dreadful sort that has so little sound. After a while it stopped, and they went on inside.

She's told him what the trouble is, Margot said to herself. Henry knows.

The thing that frightened her was the question: what would Henry do with the knowledge now that he had it? His face, before it had passed from view, had had the stiff look you associate with death masks. Or it could equally have been the inhuman expression affected, during the unique manipulation of his job, by a public executioner.

And on Friday, June eleventh, Melissa took ill. She refused to have a doctor. She went to bed.

So that was the fashion in which the stage was set.

CHAPTER 11

Saturday, June twelfth, with its curtain waiting to rise on the slow, perilous after-drama which inescapably crouches on the heels of a death by violence, broke as a scorcher.

Margot awoke to the humid discomfort of a sleep that had been fitful and had brought her no rest. The morning was an airless furnace, while the cheery sunshine crashing in through her bedroom windows seemed directly to offer itself as a parboiled insult. No wonder, she thought, that the ladies of the Southland paced their movements to the tempo of an underdone minuet.

As she bathed and dressed she tried to gather together her moist wool wits in order to face the day with a semblance of intelligence. The tableau of Francine and Henry clinging to each other down on the lawn last Thursday night had never left her. Without coming bluntly out about it, she had made an indirect attempt yesterday to touch on the incident with Henry, but he evasively had refused to rise. Melissa, ill, in bed, could not be disturbed, and Francine remained strictly aloof behind her own roadblocks of very barbed wire.

Margot reconsidered, as she had again and again, the one feeble lever which Jake had put in her hands as an instrument for trying to make the girl open up: the Hermosa Beach sequence involving Janice Heather, Jimmy Smith, and Jimmy's padlocked crypticism over his unnamed pal.

It still seemed too nebulous for any effective use, and especially so when Margot's companion thought, whenever she wavered about springing it, was a remembrance of Francine saying to her, after the bout with Bruce in the Wynstable cottage grounds: "I swear that if you try to butt in I'll do something to prevent it. Something pretty final, Miss Gilland."

That in itself made for delicate walking. On the other hand, time was running out. It was now no longer than a matter of hours to the recital, and perhaps some desperate, roughshod walking would be in order.

Revoltingly confident that she had cleverly determined nothing, Margot went downstairs for breakfast. Henry and Francine were at the table. Their greetings were much too normally in character for the bitter churning that surely was muddying their thoughts. Henry's good morning was warmly friendly, Francine's a buckram-stiffened Emily Post.

"Melissa is still rocky," Henry said. "I've called up a Dr. Ruddage and he's on his way over. According to Jarvis, he was Miss Brandgwyn's family doctor for years."

"He will be in his nineties," Francine contributed from her case-hardened groove. "And he will still be in a befuddled trance over the exciting medical miracles of nux vomica and quinine."

"Even if he is, it doesn't matter. I think Melissa is tired, that's all. She needs a rest."

He had put his foot down, Henry said, at any notion of Melissa going into Charleston tonight for the recital. She was to stay in bed. Then he wondered, while an odd overlay of tension touched his voice, whether Margot would be kind enough also to forego the concert and to stay home with Melissa.

"I'll run Francine in, Miss Gilland. I'll also do my best to serve as a net against possible brickbats."

"I'll be glad to stay—and don't worry about brickbats. There'll be none."

Margot almost missed the glance which Henry and Francine exchanged: it was so swift, and as tenuous as a flicker of light.

"Melissa will feel better with you here," Henry said. "She not only depends on you, she likes you."

Well, Margot thought, so *that* little cog has been welded into place.

Dr. Ruddage, when he came, was not in his nineties. He was in his eighties. Both from a physical and mental standard Margot thought him a thoroughly mobile general practitioner of the old school in its finest sense. She only wished there were more like him around loose.

His opinion of Melissa's condition tallied with Henry's. Her nerves simply had been on edge too long—since the initial shock to them back in California on inheriting great wealth with all of its emotionally upsetting consequences and the readjustments it had entailed. Physically, he pronounced her sound as a bell.

He gave Melissa a sedative and left her a sleeping pill which packed a bigger wallop to be taken after supper. She was to stay in bed until she was thoroughly rested, certainly for several days. No nurse was necessary, Miss Brandgwyn's old Sally being in his opinion much better than any of them—less stiff white starchiness, alarming stockings, and more earth. He would stop by again tomorrow morning.

In spite of the deadening heat the day seemed to take on an affect of acceleration, as though, so far as Brandgwyn's peculiar interests were concerned, some cosmic brake had been released and they had started helplessly to coast.

From where it lay on a console in the entrance hall Margot selected such mail as would need her attention. A copy of the Charleston *Gazetteer* was beside the letters. She carried it into the library for a check on the publicity covering the evening recital before she went upstairs.

As Margot walked into the tepid stagnation of the book-lined room she found herself faced with the last member of that small, closely interwoven group which when evening came would find themselves in hidden bondage under the clinical and cold-sweat-producing probings of those men whose official concern lay in murder.

The stranger was elderly, spare, and tall. His carriage was consciously erect, as if it were insisting upon the recognition of a military past. His hair stood in a gray brush which was more formally echoed in a clipped mustache and a swank Vandyke. His stance suggested an indifferently restrained arrogance, and only his eyes, Margot thought, betrayed a possible lack of self-confidence and a measure of being secretly on the defensive.

"Miss Gilland? I am Braintree Calverse. How do you do?"

They shook hands, and his fingers were the texture of sandpapered cypress wood. After he had ladled out an appropriate amount of regret at Melissa's being indisposed, he shifted his cumbrous attention to his wife. At the moment, he announced, she was busy over the floral arrangements in the ballroom of the Fort Sumter.

He went on: "I am waiting while Francine changes. Anne sent me to ask her to run in and give her opinion of the platform—something about the piano, the lights, the accompanist—odds and ends. We will lunch at the hotel and I shall drive her back here afterward."

Margot accepted this dose of *blague* with courteous, blank eyes. Remembering Ranger's report on the rumored shakiness of the Calverse cash, she was certain that what Braintree Calverse actually was after would be several hours during which he and his wife could get to work on Francine. This, in a bulldog determination to maneuver up to the final curtain to return Francine (plus the Brandgwyn pelf) into the hotly cordial arms of Bruce. And so save the old plantation.

But about one thing Margot did feel fairly confident: Bruce himself was straight. No matter what plush-lined bear traps his mother or his Vandyked father might be preparing to spring, Bruce would not be aware of them and certainly never consciously would have accepted a part in their setting.

The silence which had taken hold like a brooding was broken by Francine, who loomed in the doorway, somewhat like a linen-clad monitor, and said with intolerable rudeness: "I still consider this completely unnecessary, Mr. Calverse. The only possible variation to the established platform arrangement would be for the pianist to play while standing on his head."

Braintree paled from a shock of anger, but he said calmly enough: "I'm sure you're right, but Anne wishes it."

"Oh, very well."

Francine ignored Margot entirely and left, while Braintree followed, after the studied courtesies of a Southern leave-taking.

The household machinery moved inexorably on into lunch. It was a scattered meal, what with Francine being at the Fort Sumter and Henry having decided to share a tray with Melissa at her bedside. Margot, dining alone in the breakfast room, had no appetite. Her nerves were getting edgy; a state that she hoped might largely be attributed to the heat.

Henry looked in while she was having coffee and reported that the sedative had taken effect and Melissa probably would sleep during the rest of the afternoon.

Impulsively, somewhat in the fashion of grasping at a straw, Margot said: "Mr. Tyler, there is something I wish I could assure you about. It concerns the confidences that our clients sometimes have had to give us. Nothing—and I mean literally nothing—has ever leaked out, and never, certainly, has a confidence been betrayed. I wish you would believe that."

A shadow crossed Henry's face and he said gravely: "I've never thought otherwise, Miss Gilland. But there are some things—certain things that are so—"

The shadow deepened and he left the sentence hanging in the hot, quiet air. He asked whether she would please excuse him. He was, he said, going out for a walk.

Henry did not return for about two hours, and his appearance then, as Margot saw him crossing the lawn from her living-room window, gave her a shock. His shoes were mud-caked and his flannel slacks were stained (apparently from swamp water) up to their knees. A rip in the chest of an equally soiled sports shirt suggested his having forced a way through underbrush.

Later, when Margot went into Melissa's room, she found her still sleeping. Venetian blinds shuttered out the declining sun. They dimmed the figure of Miss Brandgwyn's old Sally where she sat, with the derelict immobility of age, over at a window. She stood up when Margot came in, and they talked in whispers.

"I'll take over now, Sally. Miss Francine is back and is dressing. Mr. Tyler also is dressing. You go and lie down and take a good rest, then have your dinner."

"Thank you, Miss Gilland."

"Will you let Jarvis know, please, that I'll eat here with Mrs. Tyler?"

"I shall tell him."

Evening fell, and a fractional breath of coolness touched the clammy air.

CHAPTER 12

Using the house telephone in her cottage on the Wynstable grounds, Mrs. Millay called the inn and was connected with room service.

She ordered dinner to be sent over and served as usual in the cottage patio: Maryland cream-of-crab soup, roast duckling, hashed-brown potatoes, a mixed salad, pecan pie, and coffee.

The service would be for one.

Mr. Forrest, she said, was dining out.

CHAPTER 13

Melissa did not wake up until Jarvis and a housemaid, Sarah, brought trays. Even then, although her eyes were open and she sat against the pillows, she continued to give the appearance, Margot thought, of being partially drugged. In fact, her sole moment of full awareness was when Henry and Francine came in to kiss her before they left for Charleston.

A strange moment, strange for its haunting flavor of bittersweet. With Francine no longer hard, but radiating a shy young loveliness in the gown of dairy-gold satin. "She's you, Melissa," Henry said. "She's you back then."

"Dear—dear Francine—my heart will be with you while you sing. Always with you, dear."

"Mother. We must start, Mother. I must go." Unquestionably she was crying, but her back was turned and she rapidly left the room. Henry kissed Melissa, and their eyes clung and his hand pressed hers.

He said: "Don't worry."

"No. I'm not. Truly not, Henry. Take care of her." Her voice sank so low that it was barely possible to hear her add: "And bring her back."

When Jarvis and Sarah had removed the trays, Margot asked Melissa whether she would take the sleeping pill that Dr. Ruddage had left.

"Thank you, Miss Gilland, I believe I will."

The pill was in an envelope on the bed table, and Melissa shook it out into her hand while Margot poured a glass of water from a thermos jug.

Melissa thanked Margot for the glass.

"Would you mind, Miss Gilland, letting me have that plate of peaches here beside me? So often when I wake I find one refreshing."

The plate was on a table near a window, where Jarvis had set it down, and Melissa had finished drinking the glass of water when Margot carried the fruit to the bed table. There were two peaches on the plate, a napkin, and, alongside the peaches, a paring knife that had a silver handle and a blade of hollow-ground steel.

Melissa's eyelids drooped.

Subconsciously Margot filed the thought that the pill must have been remarkably powerful for such an all-but-instantaneous drooping.

She arranged the bed pillows comfortably and then raised the Venetian blinds, letting in the evening twilight and the now somewhat less stifling air.

Not only Melissa but the world itself seemed hushed in a drowsy rest. The servants would all be at dinner in their hall in the summer kitchen, and it would be at least another hour before Sally would be back to stay with Melissa for the night.

Gentle breathing indicated that Melissa slept. In this waiting somnolence, while evening muted its twilight colors and the moon developed into a full splendor over the eastern trees, Margot's nerves accelerated their tumbling into an irritating pool of nameless concerns.

Of course Henry knew of the planned elopement—knew the nature of the hold which Forrest held to bludgeon Francine into it—he would have fewer delicacies of restraint than had Melissa toward making any move to balk the flight—had that walk in the torrid heat of the midday sun, with the torn and muddied return been an arranged step in the building of that move—just as the equivocal request at breakfast that she, Margot, forego the concert and stay home with Melissa—to be out of the way, of course—

Her cigarette case was empty. Margot left Melissa to her quiet breathing and went to her own suite to refill it. There were none. She spent a short while at the dressing table repairing the effect of the air's humidity upon her hair. Badly she needed the quieting comfort of a cigarette. She remembered that a humidor down on the library table was kept stocked with them.

The front door was standing open when she got downstairs.

The entrance-hall chandelier was on and, from the number of insects which swirled around its glow, it occurred to her that the door must have been standing open for the past several moments. The fact was puzzling. She stepped outside, and at the foot of the porch, on the moonlit gravel of the driveway, she saw the body.

With the timeless clarity of shock, she absorbed a mental photograph of the scene: Forrest Millay, clothed in a white-jacketed dinner suit, lay face down. A lazy spiral of smoke rose from a cigar that rested just beyond the reach of limp fingers. Blood, which had stopped its seepage from beneath the throat, offered its ultimate pattern of a viscous, irregular plaque on gravel.

Dead? Alive? Accident? Hemorrhage?

She went down the steps and, bending, was satisfied with a layman's assurance (in this instance she happened to be correct) that life, from the lack of a pulse in the cool, unstiffened wrist, was extinct.

She retreated to the porch, leaned back against a pillar, thought the loose, errant thought: she won't be able—she *can't* be able to sing on the red heels of this. She thought: that's silly—kill a powerful animal like Forrest, unplanned, while she wore a fragile gown of dairy gold?—very silly. But Henry?

Jarvis's voice came with its soft politeness from the doorway behind her.

"Will you excuse me, Miss Gilland, if I close this, please? There's a powerful lot of night bugs comes in when it's open."

Margot's body began to shake under a chill, emotional wind.

"Mr. Millay is dead, Jarvis. I am going to telephone. Stay here, please. Stay until the police come."

* * * *

The killer felt extraordinarily composed. Almost there was a heady sense of self-congratulation over a job well done. It was refreshing to realize there had been no hitch and that nothing whatever was left to be worried about any more.

CHAPTER 14

The atmosphere of Brandgwyn subtly changed.

Paradoxically, through Forrest's death, the house came alive. It did this neither visually nor with any faltering in its general orderliness. Rather it was as though the invisible dregs of a murder were testing their toe hold in the role of calamitous guests.

They were accomplishing this in a noxious tide which filtered its sly sampling among the halls, the rooms, the smallest cracks of age throughout the building. As a matter of more simple fact, it was well on its way toward giving the old place and the people in it a good dose of the creeps.

As soon as she was through with notifying the police, Margot telephoned Jake. His bounce, as she spoke of murder, was gone, and all of the hard qualities which underlaid the successful handling of his bizarre business came to the surface.

"Naturally the police will insist on your staying. Do you feel any sense of personal danger? I can send Ascott down to be with you—"

"Nonsense, Jake. I'll admit it shook me, but I'm all right now."

He said impatiently: "There is nothing nonsensical about a murderer. Have you any ideas on who did it?"

"Several, and I don't want any of them."

"That's exactly my point. You've grown to like the Tylers. I want you to remember this: every killer since Cain has been liked by somebody, even loved, and it never has stopped them from a repeat performance to save themselves from being found out. Just now you're one of those somebodies, and I want you to be careful, Margot."

Jake went right on. It would surely be clear to the killer that their organization would be on the job, parallel with the police, and as their representative on the scene Margot would be spotlighted out in front—a well-illuminated bull's-eye.

He would put complete pressure now on the investigation of Millay's past, both from the Pittcairn-political-machine angle and the Hermosa Beach-Jimmy Smith lead on the coast.

He wanted her, he said, to keep in constant touch, definitely to indicate her first sense of danger.

It was a disturbing mess of thoughts to carry with her as Margot hurried up to Melissa's room. For a while she stood beside the bed, looking down at the quiet, kind face profiled against the pillow. A nagging remembrance of the opened front door was insistent. Unavoidably, unwillingly, Margot was connecting it with Melissa.

Then the connection seemed hearteningly against common sense. More reasonably, one of the servants had found the body and, scared witless, had left the door standing open. That wasn't sensible either. The servant would have screamed. Inevitably they screamed. Anyhow, the servants should have been and still should be distant in their hall eating dinner.

Yet Jarvis hadn't been. Nor had he, Margot told herself with a gradually reviving hard-cooked practicality, been prowling around and self-sacrificially saving the old massa or missus or little missie from a bum rap by knocking off an about-to-press-the-doorbell guest. No, what Jarvis had been doing was exactly whatever it was he was supposed to have been doing in a house-chore line at the finish of his meal.

The windows flared under a sudden illumination of the outer night.

Looking down upon the driveway, Margot saw two powerful floodlights turning the ugly scene from a faded dusk into bright day, their electric cables snaking up across the porch to some electrical outlet in the hall. A prowl car and a small truck were parked back a ways along the drive. The truck was a mobile crime laboratory.

An ominous note lay in this lack of fanfare with which the police vanguard had arrived, in the modern efficiency and the quiet purpose with which the handful of men below her were getting on with their several concerns.

Pretty Class A for a small town such as Parnellton, she thought. Then, unhappily, she thought: too good.

"I am back now, Miss Gilland."

Margot turned from the window and faced Sally. The woman was calm. She was much too old to be shaken by anything, and certainly not by death.

"How are the servants, Sally?"

"They're excited and they're scared, Miss Gilland, but Mr. Jarvis he is toning them down. I will stay with Mrs. Tyler. Captain Strap Buran has asked me to request you to join him downstairs in the library."

Margot found the library empty.

Through the open door leading into what had been Miss Brandgwyn's office she heard the tail end of a telephone conversation, heard an unobtrusively Southern accent saying: "—so if you will call me after finishing with the Fort Sumter, I will be obliged."

Captain Strap Buran differed tremendously from Margot's preconceived picture of a Southern police chief. The picture had been an unfortunate composite, pieced together from the implications of various radio commentators who had been justifiably hot-collared over certain night-riding atrocities and, in general, hoods made out of sheets. The resulting image had cohered into a politically gross, bigoted, willfully stupid, present-day Simon Legree.

Buran was not like that at all. He had been, and still looked like, a quarterback in a first-line university team. He offered an irrational effect of daintiness both in his person and in his gestures. He did this with no loss of masculinity. Rather it was in the fashion with which a dark panther could be dainty, and you felt that Buran, within severely charted limits, could be petted.

He shook hands while he looked her over. His eyes expressed nothing. He offered the conventional gambit that it was a rotten situation, and Margot agreed.

"Jarvis tells me that Mrs. Tyler is ill, Miss Gilland. He mentioned a sleeping pill that Dr. Ruddage left for her. Did she take it?"

"Yes."

Buran struck straight to the point. He was, he said, familiar with the situation's background. Everybody was. He was referring to the Tyler-Calverse-Millay triangle with what had been its intended climax in tonight's rumored elopement. Now canceled.

"Forgive me for interrupting," Margot said, "but has anything been done about letting Mrs. Millay know? She's convalescing, and the shock might be dangerous."

He had considered that, Buran said, and it was being attended to. One of his men, a Sergeant Mattock, was at the Wynstable. Mattock was leaving it up to Mrs. Frosher to soften the blow, to be with him when he broke the news to Mrs. Millay—an analgesic that seemed a bit dubious to Margot, knowing the whalebone anatomy of Mrs. Frosher. "And Miss Tyler, Captain Buran? The recital?"

Yes, that had also been considered. Buran had been in touch with the Charleston police. He ignored the bromide that the show must go on, but said there seemed no reason or advantage in having it interrupted with unnecessary melodramatics. Miss Tyler and Mr. Tyler would be informed when it was over. He indulged in a flatly cynical, sideswipe allusion to the importance of the audience, which would be solidly composed of the county's upper crust and not, hence, judiciously disturbable.

He turned to the tedious exactitude of bracketing the moment of the crime. He had, he said, learned this much from Jarvis: shortly after seven-thirty Mr. Tyler had asked Jarvis to have a houseboy bring Miss

Tyler's convertible around to the door. As the recital was to start at nine, that would leave them plenty of time for an easy run into Charleston and the Fort Sumter.

The houseboy had left the convertible before the porch at seven forty-five, and the driveway at that moment had been devoid of Forrest. The houseboy then had returned to the servants' hall and rejoined the rest of the staff at their dinner.

Jarvis had not. He had waited to hold the door when Miss Tyler and Mr. Tyler would leave. Jarvis's sense of punctilio was fairly rigid—perhaps Miss Gilland had noticed? They had left at eight-five. Jarvis had noted the time because he had felt they were cutting the run into the Fort Sumter a little close. He had watched the car drive off before he closed the front door, and then had gone back to finish his interrupted dessert.

"We come," Buran said, "to you. At half-past eight Jarvis noticed you standing outside on the porch and spoke about the insects coming in through the doorway. About how long had you been out there?"

"Not long. Certainly I didn't think about it."

"Naturally. What brought you out there, Miss Gilland?"

"The front door—" Margot attempted to check herself but realized, now that it was too late, the stupidity of doing so. "The front door was standing open, Captain Buran." Buran thought this over.

"It doesn't make sense."

"That's what I feel. Mrs. Tyler, drugged, and myself—otherwise no one here but the servants."

"No, I know them. If one of them had found the body, there would have been an uproar. You reasoned that way too, didn't you?"

"Yes."

"About this pill that Dr. Ruddage left—"

"I gave it to Mrs. Tyler myself."

Buran looked at her thoughtfully, still sizing her up. No use in pursuing the pill subject right now, the question of whether actually it was swallowed, the time when given, the lapse before it took effect. This Gilland number would fence, parry it from her client. No, a useless effort right now.

"Let's get back to you and the porch, Miss Gilland. We can get some idea of the time length from the things you did."

She had, Margot said, seen the body, the blood. The fact of the cigar being lighted had made her consider a possible sudden seizure or stroke followed by hemorrhage, that Forrest might still be living. She had gone down, had made as certain of death as she knew how. She had retreated back to the porch, then Jarvis had spoken.

"Roughly around five minutes," Buran said. "That gives us between five after eight, when Jarvis saw the Tylers drive away, and twenty-five after eight, when you went out—say twenty minutes during which the job could have been done."

"Wouldn't the length of the cigar ash—But it's stupid of me to step into your territory."

No, Buran said, not stupid. Although actually the ash was of little value for checking the time element, unless it could be learned when Millay had lighted the cigar.

The condition of the blood was more helpful. Dr. Sellbridge, the county coroner, had just finished with his initial examination and had found indications that coagulation was starting around the pool's edge. The night was hot, and heat hastened the process of coagulation, just as cold retarded it. Also, the surface on which the blood lay was gravel, and a rough surface tended to speed coagulation, too, just as a smooth one would hold it back.

"Sellbridge feels that Millay was killed almost immediately after the Tylers drove away, Miss Gilland."

Buran left this flat enough in her lap: the possibility of Henry and Francine having driven no further than beyond Jarvis's view. Then a swift return on foot. It was a helplessly obvious consideration, and Margot left it flat too. "Just how was he killed, Captain Buran?"

"A knife. A jab in the jugular vein."

"I should think—I've done some reading on criminology—"

"Gonzales?"

"Yes, Draper—Snyder—What I'm getting at is, why wasn't there blood all over the lot, with the jugular having been cut?"

Briefly Buran considered the modern woman, the matter-of-factness with which Miss Gilland went into a subject and used words which in his mother's day would have sent a lady into a dead faint. It grated and he didn't like it, but that's the way, he supposed, these career creatures were.

"That puzzled Sellbridge too. It made him look for a blow that would have knocked Millay out before the knife was used. He found a contusion at the back of the skull." The contusion had interested Sellbridge strongly. There were certain specks embedded in it of some as yet undetermined matter, presumably associated with the weapon that had struck the blow. The laboratory men would find out what they were.

Dirt and gravel marks on the linen jacket indicated that this blow had caused Millay to crumple down on his right side. Then either a muscular convulsion or the killer had turned the body face downward. The head had been lifted and the knife sunk in. No other explanation for the blood pattern made sense.

"The lighted cigar interested you, Miss Gilland. It does me, too, but for this reason: its position in relation to Millay's outstretched hand."

Millay, Buran believed, would have been holding the cigar when the head blow was struck. Well, he had slumped down on his side. He had been turned face downward. He had been stabbed in the throat. Obviously, under those active circumstances, the cigar would have landed almost any place other than where it was found lying.

It would have been crushed under the body, or cast to the side of the driveway, but *not* calmly burning, with its ash intact and undisturbed, methodically resting beyond the fingertips of an out-flung hand as though those fingers had released it there.

"It puts the job in the amateur class," Buran said.

"What was the idea?"

"To bolster a tricky alibi is my guess. The laboratory will check the cigar."

A slightly off-balance Jarvis came in and announced that Mrs. Millay, Miss Lynndecourt, and a Miss Tishman were in the green drawing room. He explained through a thickening glaze that the ladies had been detoured by one of the officers around the criminal scene and escorted into the house by a back door. And a blot on Brandgwyn's punctilio if ever there was.

CHAPTER 15

The green drawing room offered the effect of a set piece—a static tableau sharply secluded from the principal drama going on out of doors and yet bound to it by the invisible links of grief.

An overwhelming air of repressed anguish hung about Mrs. Millay. She was seated without comfort on a chair whose background of tufted cerise satin emphasized the disease-raddled qualities of her bloodless face.

On one side of her sat Miss Lynndecourt. From her acidulous age of seventy she presented the role of a guardian escort and a spindle of strength. On the other flank Miss Tishman (fifty) suggested a pallid, ever-hoping-to-be-helpful, tasseled fringe. Straight out of stock, Margot thought. Both of them.

"I had to come, Miss Gilland," Mrs. Millay said. "I couldn't have stood it, not coming."

Freakishly, in the thick fog of this sorrow, Margot found herself engaged in formally presenting Captain Buran. It was an act acknowledged with reserved bows from Miss Lynndecourt and (an oscillating one) Miss Tishman, after which both ladies retired into their shells.

Mrs. Millay was beyond any amenities. She told Buran in a stark, crucified monotone that she wanted her son to be with her and she wanted him now. Then in a swift reversal, as though the foolish impossibility of being granted this hungry, human longing were growing clear to her, she listened patiently as Buran touched on the required formalities (he hedged around the actual word autopsy) before any funeral arrangements could be considered.

It was obvious that Mrs. Millay was on the brink of a crisis of nerves, because again her manner shifted, this time under a scald of anger. She freely admitted to a desire, to an intention of vengeance. She had small use for the more polished term: justice. Little use and less faith. Too many criminals wiggled free under technicalities in the law, or through influence or wealth.

In spite of her physical weakness and her required convalescence of rest, she seemed strong with the strength of this vengefulness. She demanded to know what she could do, what knowledge Buran needed so that quickly he could plunge the killer into that special vat of extinction she so eagerly desired.

"Well, just what were your son's plans for this evening, Mrs. Millay?"

"They were undecided. He wanted to go to the recital and yet he didn't want to. His face embarrassed him—the discolored eye, and his nose still taped because of that criminally unwarranted attack by Bruce Calverse in the drugstore. You know about it?"

"Everybody does, Mrs. Millay."

"And about the threat? I know such threats usually are nothing but the result of anger. Not meant to be taken literally. But this one was based on jealousy. People go crazy because of jealousy. Crazy enough to kill because of jealousy."

It was painfully clear that Mrs. Millay had no doubts and was determined that Buran should entertain none either. Unquestionably she was handing him Bruce, already properly manacled and trussed for an avenging gibbet. Buran declined any outright acceptance.

"We're considering everything, Mrs. Millay. Did your son finally make up his mind about the recital?"

"Not exactly. He did dress, and he told me that in any case he was going into Charleston for dinner. I got the impression he was planning to go into the ballroom after the lights were lowered. Otherwise he'd have dined at the cottage. I telephoned room service my own order."

"At what time?"

"I don't know."

"I do," Miss Lynndecourt said.

Miss Lynndecourt was neither an insensitive nor a thoughtless woman. Simply, age had made her overwhelmingly self-centered, and the tragedies of others were little more than interesting mirages on the horizon of her arid consciousness. Her regard for Mrs. Millay was entirely abstract. Certainly it wasn't solid in the sense of any valid compassion or sympathy, and her having accompanied Mrs. Millay on this tragic mission had been nothing beyond a required gesture of *noblesse oblige*.

She was trying, now, to be academically helpful, but her true concerns remained strictly personal. Such details as Buran seemed to be seeking were transposed by her into their relationship with herself.

"I remember the time," she said, "because Cloquette's supper had just been brought over from the inn kitchen, and I had set the plate down in the patio—chopped beef, a green vegetable, carrots. I could just make out your voice, Mrs. Millay, telephoning your order. Roast duckling, wasn't it?"

"Yes."

"Greasy. In Atlanta we press it. The time, Captain Buran, would have been a quarter after seven. Cloquette always dines then on the dot. Afterward she takes an hour's nap. Her digestion demands it."

"Cloquette," Miss Tishman contributed, not unhelpfully, "is a perfectly darling pug."

For one emotionally arrested second Mrs. Millay examined Miss Tishman much in the fashion of a rapt entomologist suddenly faced by a new species of offensively loathsome beetle. Then she said to Buran that Walter, her regular waiter from room service, had brought dinner and arranged it on the patio table at a quarter to eight. She did remember the hour, because Forrest had mentioned it. He had just completed dressing and was leaving.

"Miss Tishman and I," Miss Lynndecourt said, "also were starting for the inn dining room. We met on the pathway, and Mr. Millay escorted us over. We parted in the lobby, where he went to the gift counter to buy some cigars. At eight."

"You're sure that it was eight?"

"Perfectly, Captain Buran. That spineless trio which masquerades as a musical ensemble were commencing to play their opening number. A blighted rendition of one of Mr. Sousa's splendid marches."

"While he was with you did Mr. Millay say anything that might explain why he suddenly went to Brandgwyn? He definitely had started for Charleston."

"No, he didn't. We talked entirely about the hibiscus and the heat."

With an intention of getting the job finished in a lump (it was beginning to bore her), Miss Lynndecourt talked right on. She had left the inn with Miss Tishman immediately after dining because the music had been tallow-faced beyond sufferance. They had returned to the cottage. Walter had been taking Mrs. Millay's dinner tray away, and Miss Tishman had stopped him as he was heading toward the service pathway to the inn and had given him Cloquette's empty supper plate.

They then had chatted with Mrs. Millay and were with her when a police sergeant and that woman, Mrs. Frosher, had broken the dreadful news.

"There is a niche in life for everyone, Captain Buran, and Mrs. Frosher's could best be described—"

The pointed lack of enthusiasm with which Cloquette had been received by the Wynstable still tweaked. But the singular niche arranged for Mrs. Frosher by Miss Lynndecourt was never divulged. Dr. Sellbridge, the county coroner, had chosen that moment to appear in the doorway.

Much as Miss Lynndecourt had her confining absorptions, so did Sellbridge have his. They were not, however, of an egocentric character but consisted of a shelled-in preoccupation with his profession. He was a vigorous man, incessantly irritated by all the social niceties, and he had no bedside manner whatever. His sterling soundness as a surgeon alone saved him from beading hell-bent toward a pauper's grave.

He knew none of the ladies in the green drawing room, nor did he care to. They existed against his consciousness as so many disembodied, composite parts of the furniture on which they sat. Buran alone was accepted as being actively alive.

"Come outside with me, Buran, will you? I want you to see something before they cart off the works."

Mrs. Millay's cry was one of outraged anguish.

"Don't say that—don't speak of it like that—it's my son you're taking away."

This both startled and annoyed Sellbridge profoundly. He said: "We are, madam." Then he gave Mrs. Millay a sharper, a red-hot professional look. "Go to bed, madam, at once. Get your doctor to give you a pill. You're cracking. Coming, Buran?"

Buran evaded any apologies beyond a tempered suggestion to Mrs. Millay that she accept Sellbridge's advice. Then he left her, plus her bulwarking escorts, to Margot.

Mrs. Millay had grown more bloodless, if possible, than she had been. Her skin was the color of damp chalk. She stood up. In a voice which found difficulty in being articulate she regretted any inconvenience her coming had caused—if Miss Gilland would be kind enough to show them the way to their car—

Margot felt it to be a cortege she was shepherding as she routed their pomp-slow steps along Brandgwyn's back ways to Mrs. Frosher's station wagon which had brought them over from the inn.

CHAPTER 16

Margot went back to the house. The chill was getting her, straight into her bones, which should, instead, have felt uncomfortably heated by the flat, hot air. Dead as mutton, Forrest. In this, her first moment of being alone since finding him, the knowledge took on reality. But his power wasn't dead. If anything, it was stronger and worse, whatever it was, this power that had hamstrung Francine and had been causing her to fight like an ill-bred wildcat to keep it concealed.

Now it was loose. It was loose in the sense that Buran or any of his cops had the legal right to pry around and dig it out. The thought sent her running upstairs and into Francine's suite. Do it before Buran did. While he was occupied outside with Sellbridge.

It was a new experience, this searching, and she had no precedents to direct her during the short moment before Buran would be on her heels. She began with the living room.

Where hide what? Papers, most reasonably. That's what they usually were in nine cases out of ten, and, also usually, the blackmail victim hung onto them. A stupid thing, but true. A relieving possibility struck her that Francine could be as much of a novice at hiding things as Margot herself was at finding them.

Papers—desk.

A magnifying glass lay on the desk. Odd. There was nothing wrong with Francine's eyesight. It was an unusual object to own nowadays, especially for the young.

Scotch tape.

It suggested one of the most kicked-around devices of the day. She recalled a magazine article that had listed it as tops among the habits of executives for handily concealing the written-down combinations of their safes. The article had explained how pleasant this made it for burglars.

She tested it.

Taped under one of the desk drawers she found a glossy proof print. A 4 x 5.

The photograph made her sick. It was a hideously clever job. Francine, nude, alone, posed against the background of a mean room in a mean shack. (Hermosa Beach? Jimmy Smith's walking-photographer workshop?) The tattooed bust of Washington, of which Jake had spoken, standing out plain as day.

The pose was in no sense in line with the *nues artistiques* sold leeringly on postcards to tourists in the vicinity of the Eiffel Tower or at the Place de la Concorde. It was disgustingly in line with the erotic cards, the *cochons*, furtively offered by sleek *types* up on the streets and squares of Montmartre, the Place Pigalle. Obscene. Utterly vulgar, and extremely well photographed.

Most detestable of all was the fact that in no sense could Francine have been unconscious, either drugged or intoxicated, when the picture had been taken.

Instantly Margot was satisfied that the photograph had been faked.

She was familiar with the remarkable work that could be done along that line—the clever dubbing, the montage of various exposures, the retouching, infinitesimally careful in its expert perfection.

Also she knew (knowing Francine, knowing Melissa's deep knowledge of Francine's character) that never in this world would Francine willingly, consciously have posed for such a shot.

As a further assurance of this, it explained why Francine had kept the print instead of at once having destroyed it. It explained the magnifying glass.

How many miserable, bewildered, heart-sickening hours the child must have spent in microscopically examining the foul job in a pitiful effort to determine how the faking had been done. In looking for some *proof* that it had been done.

A fury swept in against the dead Forrest. The negative of this monstrosity in his possession had given him the appalling power to ruin Francine socially, professionally, and to drag her parents down with her. One copy sent to any sponsoring organization, to any agency, would smash her career and character for good. Among any society, except the most sodden, it would turn her into a pariah.

Margot's fury increased. It was not so much herself Francine would care about as it would be over the deathblow effect upon Henry and Melissa.

Well, it could be the motive for the crime with a vengeance.

A voice sounded outside the door. Buran's voice. It panicked Margot into using that favorite cache among women, favorite since the days when fig leaves, with their impractical scantiness, had become passé. She shoved the print deep in the bosom of her dress as the door opened and Buran walked in, in company with a plain-clothes man.

An edge of resentment was apparent in Buran at his finding Margot in the room.

"We both seem to have had the same idea, Miss Gilland."

"It occurred to me that Francine might have left a note, Captain Buran. In view of the rumored elopement."

Buran looked at her frostily. What a liar. What a good, simple liar. The very best thing with a lie—keep it simple.

"Did she?"

"I've found none."

He held the door open in a plain invitation for her to leave.

"We may have better luck," he said.

CHAPTER 17

Margot went to the south wing and into her living room. The angled view from its windows showed her that the driveway had been cleared. Only the prowl car was left, where it had been parked back at the curve. Burans.

She thought about Buran. She thought him a hard man, a strictly courteous one, a clever one. In line with the new style in policemen. And for the Tylers a dangerous one. She was completely conscienceless about the murder from an ethical-legal standard. Forrest had got exactly what he should have got. The crushing out of an obscene bug. An execution, really.

Still—there had been the method—the sneak blow on the back of the head, the sly lifting of the head and the considered, careful knife, the sly arrangement of the burning cigar. No righteous flare of passion was in those things. No fresh-air gust of a killing face to face, but the easy skewering of an unconscious being. Buran would look at it like that. Margot didn't want to look at it like that.

She started to take the photograph from beneath her dress, then shoved it back again. Not with Buran still in the house and free to search her rooms. Later, when he had gone, she would figure out some place to hide it for the night.

Two cars drove up and parked at the porch. The first was the yellow convertible, and she saw Francine and Henry get out and hurry into the house. The second car was a sleek job too; a club coupe of some dark color. A man in dinner clothes got out of it and followed the Tylers inside.

Margot paused at a mirror to make sure that the photograph did not show any noticeable outline under the dress yoke. She went downstairs and into the library, where the man from the coupe must have just preceded her because he was in the act of greeting Buran. Neither Henry nor Francine was there.

Buran introduced the man to her as Alberstoke Chaney, the county's district attorney.

To understand Chaney you had to accept the fact that basically he was first and always a good, practical politician. To get his job he had to be. Although his family rested solidly upon the aristocratic right, he was himself more flexible as a matter of expediency, being a good deal like a middle-aged but still spry chameleon. Ethically he had the complaisant amorality of a well-bred stoat. The next goal in his fine, blue, ripening eye was the governor's chair.

At the present moment, beneath his velvet social manner, he was good and sore. He had attended the recital with his wife and a small party of their dinner guests, and he had not been notified about this Millay mess until the recital was over. He was leery of the part which, as public prosecutor, he would have to play in it.

Socially he was of the cold front erected against the Tylers, but he remained acutely aware of the power of money and of the bulk of Melissa's inherited wealth. She could throw a high-powered string of legal talent at him that would knock him groggy.

The case was bound to be a celebrated one. From a political angle, the majority of his electors (most of whom were abysmally sub-distingué) would be rooting for the Tylers as the underdogs—as outcasts from the local snob belt by virtue of nothing more scandalous than the fact that Henry Tyler's blood was the worthy but unblue type of a good, common man. The Gobelin-tapestry effect of his skin would have nothing to do with their estimate.

As a further bedevilment, the Calverse angle also could be a sizzling platter. Very definitely so if it should develop that Bruce, in addition to having shot his hasty face off in Lindquist's drugstore, actively should have dealt himself in on tonight's unsavory stew. Neither with the Calverses nor the Tylers could Chaney afford a false step. Such as any snap accusation that an unconsulted-with Buran might bat out. It easily could backfire and kick him straight off his nicely charted gubernatorial course.

In a nutshell, he simply did not dare risk the chance of being made a monkey of. He wished with a heartfelt fervency that instead of chucking his polished aplomb around Brandgwyn, as he was doing right now, he were holed up miles away in a summer home which he maintained at Biloxi.

His greeting of Margot when Buran introduced them was admirably adjusted to his instant sizing up of her social background. Very top.

He flowed smoothly into a conversational middle ground, offering up such noncontroversial pearls as that Henry and Francine had hurried upstairs on their arrival to satisfy their concern over Melissa, and that they would descend to the library when said concern had been attended to.

That was far from all. He wanted to set the flavor of the moment, establish it in the semi-social and as little as possible in the official. Buran *must* be diverted from any possible clap-'em-in-jail frame of mind until after they would have had a good, practical talk.

The recital, he informed them, had been a magnificent success. Miss Tyler's voice would go far. Mrs. Calverse and the ladies of the committee were enchanted, and the Cecil Willisman house was assured of restoration down to its last, limp rafter.

As for Miss Tyler, already highly keyed up by the recital, the news of the shocking crime had further unnerved her cruelly. He must admit there had not been any violent outward manifestation of this emotional wrench, but Chaney could tell. Not a doubt of it.

Caught in a good, forensic clutch, he presented Margot and Buran with his personal interpretation of a Francine who, although enameled stoically, had simply been ripped to pieces on the inside. Admirably hardy about it. Most brave.

They must (this was launched on a piercing look shot pregnantly at Buran) give the dear girl time to readjust her internally displaced balance and, insofar as any immediate quizzing was required, handle her with one-hundred-per-cent kid gloves.

The object of all this fulsome solicitude brought it to a halt by coming into the library accompanied by Henry.

Even though Margot knew that Chaney had missed the real reason for it, she did concede that essentially he was right: Francine was a coldly surfaced but badly splintered youngster. And the true cause was not the murder. It was the rotten photograph, now giving a timely impersonation of the Spartan boy's dining fox, under the yoke of Margot's dress.

Buran wasted little time. He was completely free of the politic inhibitions which harassed Chaney, while still being perfectly aware that Chaney had them.

He said: "Jarvis tells me that you left for Charleston at five minutes after eight, Mr. Tyler."

"Yes, around then."

"A forty-minute run, normally."

"About."

"The Charleston police tell me that the curtain for the recital had to be held until ten after nine. What delayed you?"

Chaney cleared his throat in his best peremptory fashion and said: "The traffic is usually pretty heavy at that hour."

"No," Henry said, "it wasn't so much the traffic. It was Francine's evening bag. She'd left it behind."

They had just reached the plantation gates, he told Buran, when Francine discovered the fact. She thought that she had left it on her dresser. As Brandgwyn's driveway still retained its original narrowness from the horse-and-carriage days, he had not bothered to turn the car but had run back to the house. The bag had not been on the dresser, and after a while he had located it on a chair here in the library. On that chair over there.

"How long did this take you, Mr. Tyler?"

"I don't know. It was long enough to make us late. It and the traffic."

A clammy wave doused Margot at this open admission that Henry and Francine had been separated directly on the moment when the crime was judged by Dr. Sellbridge to have been committed. Buran's dark eyes retained their marbleized lack of expression.

"Did you look in on Mrs. Tyler?"

"No. We had said good-by. Dr. Ruddage had left a sleeping pill for her to take. There was no reason to disturb her."

There was another confusion, Buran said, and perhaps Miss Tyler would clear it up. The Charleston police had located Miss Tyler's convertible parked at the Fort Sumter. In its luggage compartment was a suitcase marked with Miss Tyler's initials.

"You know perfectly well, Captain Buran, that I had made plans to elope."

"Yes, it's why they thought it was funny. That the suitcase felt light enough to be empty. It was unlocked. They found nothing but a large roll of one-inch adhesive plaster in it, Miss Tyler."

The inference that a roll of surgeon's tape was odd equipment for an elopement hung like a patient threat in the room's fermenting silence. Margot could feel sweat starting on her forehead. Chaney could feel sweat starting on his.

Henry's tan turned liverish and he seemed on the point of speaking when Francine, with unbelievable composure, said indifferently that it was perfectly simple. Their plans—Forrest's and hers—had been fluid. Possibly to stay in Maryland for a while—possibly to return at once to Parnellton. She had thrown the suitcase into the car for things she had expected to buy when their minds were made up.

"I'm still wondering about the roll of surgeon's tape, Miss Tyler."

"So am I."

It had been left in the bag, Francine thought, when they had reached here from the coast. Accidentally so. Her ankle had been sprained during the journey—she had taped it for a while—and that was all.

And it was also hideously thin. It had the brassy spuriousness of a party platform plank, and certainly Buran wasn't taken in. Naturally Chaney wasn't either (there was nothing the matter with his brains), but he seized on it smoothly as a not too moronic escape before any more rabbits were produced and he would have had his imperative private talk with Buran.

"Captain, Miss Tyler must be desperately worn out and grievously upset over this shocking death of her fiancé. Need she, or Mr. Tyler, be any further disturbed this evening?"

Buran was satisfied. He had about what he wanted at this preliminary stage of the job. The Tylers, father and daughter, were lying. Whether to save one or the other's neck didn't matter, nor did it if their hands were innocent. They had guilty knowledge of some aspect of the crime, that much was positive. As positive as his conviction that Miss Gilland had it too.

For all practical purposes, the Tylers were shackled to Brandgwyn through the desirability of wearing a guiltless front, and Buran saw no need for being officially obvious and making the chains any stronger.

Furthermore, there were the other avenues to explore. In a sense they could be even more significant than the Tylers, although this, right then, he seriously doubted. Bruce Calverse was one—even the old gentleman Braintree with his rumored teetering on the edge of financial ruin. There were the material minutiae now starting under test by the laboratory men, in particular the specks of foreign matter in the contusion, and the cigar. Finally, a careful digging up of Millay's reasonably immediate past.

No, there would be no harm in letting the stuffed windbag (one of Buran's more flattering opinions of Chaney) have his way. Chaney obviously was after a private talk, and what its tenor would be was anything but obscure to Buran.

He agreed. He said that he would leave Patrolman Fleury at Brandgwyn as an overnight protection against conceivable if indeterminate dangers. He said this with a courteously blank face.

Then he added his good nights to Chaney's.

CHAPTER 18

The departure of Chaney and Buran did nothing to freshen the heavy atmosphere in the library. If anything, it thickened, like a dark screen that the Tylers were arranging to mask themselves from Margot. She caught the very clear impression that both of them were afraid of her. Francine had the look of a statue frozen stiff, and she said in a tight voice: "There will be nothing more tonight. No talk. Nothing." She left them.

"I'm going up with her," Margot said.

"No." Henry's voice was final. It clung with difficulty to the thin edge of politeness. "She is better alone, Miss Gilland. Sometimes things just get too much. I'm going to send Sally to bed. I want to sit with Melissa and tell her about this when she wakes up. Break it to her easy." Henry hesitated at the door and looked back. "I know what the score is right now. I know it exactly, Miss Gilland. I don't suppose that Captain Buran—I don't suppose that when he was talking with you—"

"No. Nothing, Mr. Tyler."

"Well, I'll say good night, then.

The house settled down.

Patrolman Fleury arranged his beefy person on one of Brandgwyn's museum-piece *fauteuils* near the stairway in the entrance hall. His big, phlegmatic face was an unkind mask that concealed the liveliest sort of an imagination, and he firmly believed that his eyes resembled and were equivalent to those of a lynx.

He squeezed a paper-covered edition from a hip pocket and entered with pleasure into the spirited adventures of Highball Harry—meticulously mustached *bon vivant*, a *conoscente* to his manicured fingertips, second-story man to the elite—in general, a rapier rogue with a heart as big as all get-out.

Margot's good night to Fleury as she went upstairs was answered with a guttural mumble apparently expressed in Ro—H.H. being involved at the instant in loosing a stomacher of Lady Thyngwort's rocks under a set of trying circumstances which, for a lesser man, would have spelled mud.

In the relieving privacy of her rooms Margot took a good look at the night's mess. The only sensible course was to go straight to Francine and talk the problem over frankly. Tell the girl that Jake would take over, would submit the abominable photograph to the best available expert and find out just how it had been doctored. Once that was determined, the poison largely would have been taken from its sting.

But Francine just now was in no emotional condition for coherent reasoning. She was as near to being off her track as you could get without modeling a straitjacket. The morning would be better. Also there was Henry's emphatic No. It could be he had wanted to leave the field clear for himself. For himself to join Francine, then together to spend the night in feverish planning and their private nightmare of doubts and indecisions.

Very strongly she wanted to telephone Jake, but a mental image of the darkly mumbling Fleury on guard below disposed of that. Very much on guard, in spite of Buran's euphemism about protection. She could picture the man's breath hot on her neck as she lifted the telephone.

She took the photograph from her dress while realizing that her possession of it, until she could send it by plane to Jake, was as dangerously explosive as when it had been in Francine's keeping.

She considered where to hide it, ruling out the desk, as well as some more unique places of which she had read—such as rolling it up in a window shade. There were no window shades, just Venetian blinds.

She began to realize that she was dead tired and that her head was getting the consistency of a bowl of dough. With a grandmotherly simplicity, she moved a chair at one corner of the living room's large rug, put the print under the rug, and replaced the chair in its original setting.

She went to bed.

But not at once to sleep: Henry mentally was with her, his having gone for a walk in the blaze of the midday sun, then his muddied, shirt-torn return. Henry, who surely knew of the photograph. What else more desperate would account for that utter breakdown, that hopeless clinging to him by Francine, down on the lawn last Thursday night? It was more than enough to have sent him hotfoot after Forrest's throat. But slyly? The careful, judicious sliding of a blade into the jugular of that helpless throat?

Melissa, naggingly, insistently, was with Margot too. In connection with the opened front door. And Buran's thorough interest in the door and in whether Melissa definitely had taken the sleeping pill. Margot was perfectly familiar with the bald-headed old ruse of the sleeping-pill routine—give someone a sleeping pill—he sleeps but (surprise!) he's wide awake because he hadn't swallowed the pill after all. And Buran would be familiar with the routine too.

Uneasily she remembered that her back *had* been turned while Melissa presumably had been downing it. Also the fact that Melissa, for the most trivial sort of reason, had chosen just that moment to ask for the transferring of the plate of peaches.

Then, when she had gone to her own rooms for cigarettes, had Melissa rendezvoused with Forrest?

Had the paring knife beside the peaches, with its silver handle and blade of hollow-ground steel, been the tempting weapon?

And had Melissa, darting back upstairs into bed, left the front door standing open in her panicky haste?

Rats—elegant, nonsensical rats!

This visioned scampering around in a murderous role of steady, wonderful, calmly lovable Melissa was too much.

Margot slept.

* * * *

The killer did not sleep, for the edges of complacency were wearing thin. The period of speculative doubts was starting to germinate. What had not been done to assure the letter-perfect fashion of the crime? What had been done that should not have been done? What little thing?

CHAPTER 19

The night, in its stillness, moved on.

Patrolman Fleury finished accompanying Highball Harry on a concluding escapade which covered a posh lifting of the filthy old Pasha of Dharwikistan's pecan-sized emeralds. He shut the book upon Harry's virtuous pledge that one half the profit of the fenced loot would be sent anonymously to the Society for Underprivileged Derelicts. The destination for the other half was, of course, too silly to mention.

Fleury stood, stretched, and lumberingly catfooted his way back to the summer kitchen where a pot of coffee had been left for him on the stove.

Upstairs, Margot woke.

It was pitch night. The moon had set, but no touch of false dawn as yet showed to soften the jet curtain of the sky.

Faint, distantly spaced sounds were recognizable out in her living room. They were not decisive. They could be man-made, or they could be old-house-made. They could be the gropings of a searcher in the darkness. In spite of his appearance of overstuffed vacuity, the thought of Fleury being on watch down below was a comfort. Margot lighted the bed lamp

A crashing realization of the photograph, of the dangerous responsibility which she had assumed by having taken it, brought her fully awake. It drove her into slippers and out into the living room. She snapped on its ceiling lights. The room was undisturbed. There was no one to see.

In spite of this, her muddy worry lingered. She retrieved the picture from beneath the rug, turned out the ceiling lights, and went back to bed. She shoved the print under her pillow and, feeling better about its security, switched off the bed lamp.

In the dark quiet which lay tremulant with all the small privacies of the unseen, she drowsed back toward the deep sleep from which she had wakened. Before it enveloped her, while still on the fringes of consciousness, to bolster her wish for reassurance she slid her hand beneath the pillow in order that it might rest upon the print. It did not. It rested on a hand.

Her flash effort at a scream was choked off by the clamping of fingers about her throat. The fingers were strong. Margot was strong too. In the pitchy dark, after her first paralyzing effect of sheer terror, she fought back.

She broke the hold. More deadly than the attack itself was the complete silence that followed, the lack of any immediate recurrence of it, the senseless, utter cessation of this attempt to kill her.

The very shock of this oddity delayed the scream for help that again was welling in her battered throat, and then, in this instant of fearful hesitation, from below her on the floor beside the bed, she heard the terrible, frustrated sound of inexperienced sobbing. There was a hopelessness in it, so deep, so wretched with despair that it could not be plumbed. She turned on the bed light and knelt on the floor beside Francine. Tentatively she put an arm around her.

"We must talk."

Francine shook the arm off and stood up. Her tears dried under the heat of a returning belligerence that was largely fear.

"What's there to say? You've seen it."

"That picture was faked."

"You think so?"

"I know so."

"How was it done?"

"I don't know, but we'll find out."

The belligerence in Francine's look began a wary retreat.

"You can guess how it knocked me out when I found it was gone."

"Yes. I'd have acted just as you did."

"I knew it wasn't the police. If they'd taken it they'd have done something about it. That left you."

"Luckily."

"I was in the living room when you woke up."

"I heard you."

"I guess I went crazy when your hand slid over mine under the pillow."

"That was natural. I know what you've been going through. Let's forget it."

"All right. And thanks." Francine nodded toward the pillow. "What can you do about it?"

"I'll send it by plane in the morning to Mr. Harden. He'll have an expert examine it."

Francine flushed a hot red.

"He will know it's me."

"Yes, but look at it like this—as a necessary operation. It will be absolutely impersonal. Surely you can believe that?"

"Well, when you think of it that way."

"He'll want to know all he can about it."

"What sort of things?"

"Take the background. It looks like a room in a shack. Was it Jimmy Smiths workshop at Hermosa Beach?"

"You've been checking up pretty thoroughly, haven't you?"

"I was hired to. You're sensible enough to know it wasn't prying."

"Yes, I can see that. And you can see now why I didn't want you to."

"Perfectly. Was it Jimmy's shack?"

"I don't know. I knew he had one, but I never saw it."

"Then that is one part of the faking."

"You're believing me."

"Of course I am."

"I've not been especially nice to you, like being pleasant."

"Nobody in your situation could have been. Let's stick to the print. Were you ever any place alone with Jimmy? Indoors, I mean."

"No."

"But he did take your picture?"

"Yes, several times while he and Janice and I were on the beach. I guess you know about Janice?"

"Yes. Did you keep on seeing him after she was laid up with the flu?"

"No, because we were getting ready to move East—but, Miss Gilland—"

"Yes?"

"After the publicity broke about Miss Brandgwyn's will, Jimmy did start shooting an awful lot of pictures of me. Not with Janice in them, just of me alone. He kidded about my having become a celebrity, sort of made a gag about it. Clowning."

"How about that friend of his who wanted to meet you? Did you meet him?"

"No."

"Have you ever thought about him in connection with Forrest? About there having been a connection between Jimmy Smith and Forrest?"

"I know there must have been." A flash of unspeakable hatred shook Francine. "I wish he could be killed again."

"Don't ever say that!"

"I won't. But I wish it. I wish it very much. He died too quick." It felt better being off her chest, and Francine said more calmly: "I'm not worrying about your telling the police. I did worry. I guess that's why I did what I did."

"I've said that was forgotten. What we do have to worry about is whether Mr. Harden's agents can beat the police in locating the negative and any duplicate copies. They'll have to cover the Los Angeles end and Cleveland. They'll have a head start in those two places but they certainly won't right here—in the Wynstable cottage. Buran's probably having it taken apart tonight."

"That's all right. There wouldn't be any in the cottage."

"Why not?"

"Forrest never would have kept anything there. Because of his mother. He wouldn't have risked it."

"I don't quite see that."

With a resurgence of acid bitterness, Francine used a scalpel on Forrest.

"He told me if even a hint of his rotten blackmail rackets got to her he'd kill me. And he said he'd see to it that a copy of the print got to Mama and Papa after I was dead. He had a fix on her, on her thinking about him as a tin god. That's why I'm sure it's all right about the cottage."

"You said rackets?"

"That's right. I wasn't the only one. Just the last."

"Funny he should tell you about the others."

"No, why wouldn't he? He had me. He had me so helpless that he could tell me anything and know I'd keep still about it."

"Even so. It isn't quite sensible."

"He wasn't sensible. I mean at times. He was a periodic lush. He got drunk one night and talked. It was a form of conceited boasting, I guess. Do you want any of it?"

"All of it."

When put in connected digest, it was not any parlor story. And always in the back of Margot's mind, while Francine talked, lay the thought that it had been Forrest's own version of his past and as such it could be true, or partly so, or completely false.

His father had been a moderately important party-machine man in Pittcairn's notorious setup. When around with the boys and in his political ward work, he had been the jolly, good-old-likable, perfect brick. But at home he had been a stinker, and finally Mrs. Millay had left him, taking Forrest with her. Shortly after this separation he had died. That had been ten years ago.

Mrs. Millay had got a job as housekeeper on the Adirondack estate of a wealthy bachelor, a Silliman Corning. The estate covered several thousand acres in the Loon Lake district, and Forrest's boyhood had been spent there, with Corning treating Mrs. Millay and Forrest rather as members of the family than as employees.

Evidently he had been fairly well gone on Mrs. Millay, because, on his sudden death, it turned out he had left her the residue of his estate. This, after everything was settled, had not cut up into much. Great properties of that period had begun to take on the nature of white elephants. Nobody wanted them, and the Adirondack place practically had had to be given away to a foolhardy small combine of witless dreamers who had thought they could make a boys' camp of it.

Forrest had been forced to fish around for an opening that would bring in cash. The one which appealed to him as promising the least headache had been to lean on his father's past connections and brace Pittcairn for a job. He had told Francine that his mother hadn't liked the idea especially, but he had insisted.

Pittcairn had been agreeable. ("He liked my looks, and figured he could use them," Forrest had said.) As for the nature of the job, that was where the slugs of scotch that Forrest had downed had made him loosen up so boastfully, so recklessly in his talk with Francine.

The scheme had consisted in the operation of a somewhat unusual form of blackmail. In it Forrest would arrange to hang something unspeakably off-color on certain wealthy, respected, influential men of state-wide repute. He would do this either directly or through their wives or some other member of their immediate family. The payoff being that they would then be pressured into delivering their backing and support to some machine candidate who would be coming up for election.

Money was never accepted from the victims or demanded: simply the vote-getting prestige of their endorsement, and at times nothing beyond the comparable value of their silence. Forrest's personal take had come directly from the machine in the form of a salary, in agreeably flexible expense accounts, and in bonuses.

Mrs. Millay had not known, had not faintly suspected any of this. She had been far too ill during that period to grasp anything very clearly or, so far as that went, even to try. Forrest had led her to believe that he was being held under wraps and being groomed for important things, for some plum that was to be handed him when the war ended. Well, the war had ended and a reform wave had thrown the Pittcairn machine out on its scabrous neck in the permanent role of a non-revivable duck.

At which point of information, Francine said, Forrest had passed out.

"Nice, wasn't it? Nice fellow."

"Look, Francine, you're wasting time by keeping up this bitterness against him, and we've no time to waste."

"I know it. He's dead."

"To get back to Jimmy Smith—have you kept any of the beach snapshots he took of you?"

"Yes, about a dozen."

"Jake will want them."

"For comparison? Don't you think I've done that? Night after night going nuts?"

Francine hadn't, Margot said, done it the way Jake would have it done. The best technician in the country would be given the job of determining the method of the flimflam and of establishing expert testimony of its existence.

"Francine—does your father know?"

"Yes, but Mama doesn't. And I haven't let him see the picture. I just told him how shameful it was and that it had been faked. I'd die before I'd let him see it. And I'd die twice before letting Mama see it."

Margot studied the drawn young face, and the cruelty of any further questioning was obvious. Not only the cruelty but the senselessness of it. What was there to ask beyond a bald: did your father kill? Did you? Or: what did you see when you were left alone in the car while your father went back to the house for your bag? Was it Bruce Calverse you saw? The boy you truly love? Was the murder a thing already done when your father left the house again? When he rejoined you in the car was he pale and cold from the sly butchery he had seen? Did he shield you from it by sick silence?

Absurd now. Absurd ever to ask them, as a matter of fact. They held no answer that the child would give.

"Go to bed now, will you? You won't get any real rest. You couldn't, of course. But you will know there's some hope, that something practical is going to be done about the picture."

"Thanks, Miss Gilland. Margot."

* * * *

Finally, having dismissed for the moment all gnat-like, worrisome speculation, the killer slept. It was a deep sleep and it held no dreams beyond dim images in shadow along the hem of some casual memories that had, during wakefulness, been long forgot. Day broke and a hot sun rose behind a swatch of crimson streamers banding the eastern sky. After a while the killer rose too. And after a while the killer's thoughts— although as yet with a negligent sort of idleness—turned in their refurbished clarity toward Margot.

CHAPTER 20

The morning being Sunday, the press had no editions in which to herald the Tyler-Millay job (Brandgwyn Heiress—Slaughtered War Hero), with its tailor-made, sob-sister tangents of the damped-out elopement and of Bruce, jilted scion of the socially prominent Calverses. On the other hand, the radio was pleased, and its nation-wide newscasts did a well-browned coverage.

Brandgwyn itself was in no sense pleased.

An air of unbearable expectancy underlay its surface routine which barely managed to run along with a sketchy semblance of normal equilibrium. Small details alone betrayed its true state of nerves—the open salts being poltergeisted into sugar—a dust-cloth absent-mindedly left swaddling a marble bust of Theodosius the Great—such minor things.

Girded in a dress of cool checked cotton for what was bound to be a jaw-buster morning, Margot went down to breakfast at eight. She had expected it to be a solitary meal, but it was not. The family was entirely there.

Melissa looked her own quiet self except for a touch of puffiness about her eyes and, in them, a hint of the miserable anxiety which she was controlling with firm success. Henry was semi-formalized in white linen, a dove-toned shirt, and a subdued orchid-crepe tie. His expression was soberly masterful, and Margot wondered about it until a probable explanation came to her.

Under the weight of tragic circumstance, he was once more the head of the house, the bulwark of strength against which his wife and daughter could trustfully lean. It was the role he had played with such staunch, good kindness until the Brandgwyn money had sledge-hammered its base into silly bits and had left him dangling with all the inoperative and bootless feelings of an empty figurehead.

Francine (frosted in pique) looked a studied blank. Margot saw no ravages from what must have been a sleepless night, and her greeting blended indistinguishably with Henry's while Jarvis—already crowding sail toward the jitters—held Margot's chair.

"Miss Gilland," Melissa said with her effect of wholesome directness, "Henry wanted me to but I refused to stay in bed. I am quite well, truly well, and I know what we shall be called upon to face. It will be an unhappy repetition of Cousin Elizabeth's bequest."

It took a moment for this to make sense. "Oh—you mean the press." It was peculiar, more than just peculiar, Margot thought, that reporters should be uppermost in Melissa's mind rather than any probings about the crime on the part of Buran or Chaney. *Could* even Melissa feel as assured-of a security-in-innocence in her husband and her daughter as all that? No, it wasn't peculiar. Of course Melissa both could and would.

"Yes, Miss Gilland. We were wondering whether you could see the interviewers for us."

"I could, but I don't think it would be wise, Mrs. Tyler. I'd even suggest my staying deliberately out of the picture."

Henry said: "What Miss Gilland is getting at, Melissa, is for us not to antagonize them or act as if we were being coached. We're bound to get a bum pitch, but there's no sense in making it worse. They've already doped out their own conclusions as to how things are. If we're friendly, maybe they'll soft-pedal it." He looked levelly at Margot. "That's it, isn't it?"

"I'm afraid it is."

"Those big-time buzzards," Francine stated flatly, "wouldn't soft-pedal the last-act rattles of a dying Mimi." That was not, Margot insisted, entirely true. On the other hand, when receiving them, there was no necessity for going overboard on the friendly act—and this would definitely hold true with the news photographers.

She warned them against either being bullied or painlessly eased into poses of an unsympathetic, undignified, or trick nature. She pointed out that the shots would have syndicate coverage and that while the good will of the press was valuable, the sympathy of the public could, under certain eventualities, become more so.

"You know the type of thing I mean—the President of the United States posed in Apalachee turkey feathers or gazing with dignity into the eyes of a wet trout. Well, if they want anything in similar bad taste, be polite and agreeable but be firm—just don't do it."

"And how," Francine asked, "with those cheesecake-besotted mackerels, do you go about just not doing it?" Margot said acidly: "You tell them with a wistful smile, even if the shock permanently dislocates your lips, that you simply wouldn't feel natural. You then take a cemented stand beside that spinet in the green drawing room. If you have one, hold a sheet copy of some Stephen Foster number in your maidenly fingers so that the title will register, then let them shoot. And in that, Francine, I'm serious."

Henry smiled and said: "And me?"

"Always with Mrs. Tyler. Side by side."

"I get it, Miss Gilland. Thanks."

The rest of the breakfast was a hideous, artificial strain. Jarvis was largely present during it, but even if he had not been, Margot knew that the lid had been clamped tightly on any discussion of the murder.

Curiously, it was Henry who saved the moments from falling into the agony of a flat silence. He stuck doggedly to the general subject of publicity, carrying them through the last drop of coffee with an amusing comparison between the methods of ballyhoo in favor during his carnival years and as it was handled today.

After the grim meal was over Margot borrowed Francine's car and drove to the inn. With her, sealed in a heavy manila envelope, were the blackmail print and the snapshots which Jimmy Smith had taken of Francine at Hermosa Beach.

Using the inn's dial telephone, in its privacy-yielding booth, she called Jake at his apartment, telling him of the print and of the information which Francine had given her of Forrest's (his version of it) past. It being Sunday and the post offices closed, she thought the time element important enough to send a messenger with the prints directly to Jake by chartered plane.

"Do it," Jake said. "The question of the faking has got to be settled before the police get onto the extortion angle." He was silent for a moment and then said bluntly: "My bet's on Henry. What's yours?"

"Jake, it doesn't matter. I'm about sick over it."

"Don't get me wrong. My sympathies are with him as well as the bet. That slimy, beautiful milk shake deserved exactly what he got. We'll do everything we can to save Tyler's neck."

There were, Jake said, some additional pieces of information which had come in since their last talk. Davis, during his investigations in Pittcairn's home town, had found that a Hillgrove Millay had been connected with the party machine. He had died ten years ago, and these facts, Jake pointed out, checked with Forrest's story to Francine.

Davis had looked up this Hillgrove Millay's death certificate. The man had been born in New Franconia,

Michigan, a village with a present population of 1,190 people. Davis was there now. Just what Davis might dig up neither Jake nor Davis knew.

Jaffries's report from Los Angeles was of a more startling, and possibly a more significant, nature. Jaffries had arranged an appointment to meet Jimmy Smith on Friday evening—the night before last. He had gone to keep it at Smiths photography salon on the Strip. Well, the salon was closed—out of business—and Smith had disappeared.

After a while Jaffries did root out a lead that Smith was understood to have gone to Guaymas, Mexico, with the cautious intention of taking a prolonged rest cure down there in the Pacifico Hotel.

"Jaffries is flying to Guaymas this morning, Margot—and I'll give you a ring the moment the job's done on the print."

They said good-by, and Margot drove on to Charleston's airport. She arranged for a courier and a charter plane to handle the manila envelope, and for them to start at once.

CHAPTER 21

From the number of cars parked along Brandgwyn's drive it seemed that the press had taken over. Margot left the convertible at the garage and went into the house by the back way.

Buttonholing Jarvis in the butler's pantry, she learned that Dr. Ruddage had come, had given Melissa a checkup, and had gone. Further data: one of Buran's men was questioning the staff in the servants' quarters, and Bruce Calverse was passed out cold in an upstairs guest room.

Concerning the press, Jarvis's report on their activities showed that his poise was rapidly growing nonexistent. "Every room downstairs here, Miss Gilland, like they was owning Brandgwyn and all our bodies and souls and with their camera lights just like fireflies popping. Even, they drove me into standing out on the porch and pointing at the spot where Mr. Millay fell last night."

"About Mr. Calverse—did he—did the reporters—"

"No, Miss Gilland, they don't know he is here."

Bruce, it appeared, had ignored the last curve in the driveway and, after passing through a hibiscus hedge, had then given the car its head. He had come to a stop in the vegetable garden among the leeks. He had requested an audience with Miss Francine. The audience had been taken over by Henry, who, with the assistance of Jarvis and a houseboy, had hoisted Bruce up the back stairs and onto a bed. There the eclipse had become total.

With the intention of a brief freshening before she faced the reporters, Margot herself went up the back way. The usual flat calm of the upper hall was murmurous with fragmented talk seeping up from below. It was less murmurously broken by Bruce's voice coming at her from an open doorway.

"Miss Gilland, I—I seem to have mislaid my shoes," Margot looked in. It would have taken clairvoyance right then to identify Bruce as an accepted member of the gilded South. His dinner jacket was soiled into several unfashionable shades off white, being closer to the tone known as spotted oyster. His good looks still glowered, but in an un-authoritative way, while his shock of dark hair suggested in its coiffure that explosive originality so uniquely to be found in a certain Hollywood columnist's celebrated hats.

"Jarvis probably put your shoes in the cupboard, Mr. Calverse. I'll see."

"No, no—permit me."

Bruce made a gallant gesture at rising from the edge of the bed, himself to track down the missing shoes. It was not a success.

"Here they are," Margot said.

"Most kind." Bruce put the shoes on. "I wonder if I could have some water—"

Margot drew a glassful in an adjoining bathroom. "Thank you, Miss Gilland. We will now hope for the best."

"Would you like Jarvis to bring up some coffee?"

"No, thank you. And now where is Francine?"

"It will be some time before she can see you, Mr. Calverse."

"Look—let me assure you—"

"No—please—I don't mean you. It's just that right now she is being interviewed and is posing for the news cameramen."

It was remarkable how instantaneously Bruce sobered. "That's why I'm here. To be beside her. I would have come last night, only I drew a complete blank. From around five in the afternoon straight on."

"Have you ever before?"

"Yes, just once. During a leave in London. My first leave, as a matter of fact. It was the letdown, probably. And yesterday it was that rotten elopement getting closer every minute."

"Does Captain Buran know this, Mr. Calverse?"

"Yes. He and Chaney came around this morning. I've just left them back at the house."

"Obviously, as you were in a blank-out, there was nothing you could tell them."

"I know, but there were a few things that Buran could tell me. Funny the way things piece together, and it's grim to hear about them—like hearing stuff about a total stranger when all the time you know it's you. Tell me, do I look like Lochinvar?"

"You could. But as of this moment, no. Not unless his horse had been practicing back-flips with you in the swamp."

"Bad as that?"

"Not really. What's this sudden latch on young Lochinvar?"

"Me. Here's what Buran told me, Miss Gilland. He put it together from odds and ends picked up by the Charleston police last night. He told me I reached the Fort Sumter taproom around six o'clock. I don't remember doing so. I don't remember a thing after five o'clock, when I finished dressing at home."

"Doesn't Mrs. Calverse—or your father—"

"Oh yes, and they insisted to Buran that I seemed quite all right. A little morose—Mother's description—capably three sheets in the wind—Dad's—and that I got in the jeep and headed for Charleston."

"It's fantastic to me how anyone who is blanked-out can drive."

"Perfectly fantastic, utterly unadmirable, and dangerous, but they do. I did. At the Fort Sumter—this is according to Buran—I shortly became the bosom pal of several absolute strangers. The police were given a cold-blooded account of my plans for the evening by one of them—a buyer in cotton from Dallas."

"The Lochinvar motif is beginning to make sense."

"Exactly, only with the jeep doing a substitute for the dope's horse. They say I told these spellbound pals that my avowed intention—my language was described as being a combination of the gadzooks and overripe Limehouse—anyhow, the plot was to snatch my lady from a slavering wolf's jaws and marry her myself. Something like that. Of course there was the inevitable threat mixed up in it too. Slit the wolf's throat—that sort of thing."

"It isn't good."

"I know. My exit line from the taproom was delivered at seven. A lulu."

"Did you take the jeep?"

"Yes. The parking attendant reported having ladled me into it. And from then on, until I woke up dead in my bed at home this morning, the report is a blank. Do you know something, Miss Gilland? I'm glad of it."

"Because of the Tylers? The crime having been done here?"

"Yes. It takes a lot of pressure off them. Any chump could figure out that my blanking-out was just so much boloney, faked up as an alibi, and that I did the job."

"After stating in the taproom you were going to?"

"That could be put down as just so much more camouflage. I even had a knife with me. A penknife. Buran asked me to let him have it. Laboratory stuff, I guess—testing for traces of blood."

"Has he restricted you in any way? Sticking around town, that sort of thing?"

"No, but I think he would have if it hadn't been for Chaney. Chaney and Mother went in for a mutual pooh-pooh-pooh act which you could tell made Buran good and disgusted. I guess you appreciate how Chaney operates—politics, politics, lay off the moneybags and the county aristocracy. Tell me, Miss Gilland, just when would you say I could see Francine?"

Margot felt uncomfortable. The sickening, shameful existence of the salacious photograph would keep, as it had kept, an impassable barrier between the two of them until the print's faking was unquestionably determined. Francine would see to that.

"Mr. Calverse, she is in a bad state of nervous strain, and I'm positive it would be best, that it would be kinder, if you just left a message. Seriously—please don't try to see her before tomorrow at the earliest."

Bruce's expression lost its amiability and grew stubborn. "Sorry, Miss Gilland. No dice."

CHAPTER 22

With the departure of the press a lethargy of bleak foreboding clamped on Brandgwyn.

Bruce had gone, and it had not been a pleasant departure. He had waited upstairs for Francine, only to have her completely ignore him and lock herself in her suite. For a disgraceful moment he had pounded on her living-room door, only to hear her scream at him from its other side to go away, to leave her alone, and finally, at Henry's insistence, Bruce had gone.

The coma was broken at four in the afternoon by Buran, who came in upon Margot in the library. With her urgent wanting to hear Jake's report on the photograph, she had drawn some nervous satisfaction from hovering within earshot of the telephone.

Buran said good afternoon, that he had come to see Mr. Tyler, that Jarvis had gone upstairs to tell him.

"Stay here, please, Miss Gilland. I want to talk with you afterward."

Henry, when he joined them, had the look of just having been dragged from a sound sleep, and his greeting of Buran fell far below the hospitable.

"No sleep last night," he said. "I'm bushed."

It was not in Buran's nature, either, to fiddle around or to play the smart aleck with setting traps. He thought them overrated, generally a failure and very much a waste of time.

He said: "Mr. Tyler, the servants have been talking about the walk you went for yesterday. They thought it a crazy thing for you to do because of the midday heat. They were puzzled by the condition of your clothes when you came back—the tear in your shirt, the general muddiness.

Henry was very awake now.

"I'm not used to swamps, Captain."

Buran ignored this.

"There's a dilapidated cabin in the swamp standing on an island of firm ground. During the early plantation days it was used as a place for the solitary confinement of disobedient slaves. They would be locked up in it until they came to their senses. Your wife would know about it from her childhood days here with Miss Brandgwyn."

"I see what you're after, Captain. She told me about it, yes. I'd been thinking of it off and on as a possible place to use for keeping in practice. Yesterday Mrs. Tyler was in bed, Francine lunching with the Calverses in Charleston, and Miss Gilland busy. So I looked the cabin up."

"The case of twelve knives in it is the one from your carnival act, Mr. Tyler?"

"That's right. I got it and left it there."

"After you had inspected the cabin?"

"Yes."

"During which trip did you miss the path and soil your clothes?"

"On my way back from having left the knives."

"There are two ringbolts screwed into a log of the wall near the ceiling. Sometimes a slave's wrists would be lashed to them as a special punishment."

"Yes, I noticed them."

"Mr. Tyler, I'm not going to insult you by beating about the bush. When you returned with the case of knives you also brought a fresh-cut length of new clothesline. It is lying on the floor beneath the ringbolts. The roll of surgeon's tape which Miss Tyler put in her empty suitcase was an afterthought. The suitcase, of course, was to lull any suspicions on Millay's part that she had no intention of going through with the elopement."

"You're taking a good deal for granted, Captain."

Buran said impatiently: "A child could figure out the setup, sir. The plan to elope by plane was canceled after Mrs. Tyler's present of the car. Your daughter's arrangement with Millay was that she would get away from you during the usual crush at the end of the recital and would meet him in the parking lot. They would start at once, but you would have left the ballroom much earlier and would then be concealed in the luggage compartment."

"What is the use of this when—"

"I know. When he was killed right here shortly after eight. I'll get to it, Mr. Tyler. This is what would have happened. Somewhere along the coastal highway your daughter would have made an excuse to stop the car and you would have taken over. With Millay lashed to the ringbolts in the cabin and his mouth taped to keep him from crying out, you would have reduced him to a state of terror by hurling knives at him until he gave up whatever the hold was he had on Miss Tyler."

Henry seemed turned to stone. Margot for some time had been turned to stone. For a moment Buran waited in patience.

Then he said: "Are you now more willing to co-operate, sir?"

After a moment Henry said: I'm not going to insult your intelligence either, Captain. I don't understand you. What do you expect me to do? It's of no consequence whether the things you speak of were true or not, because they didn't occur. And if they were, do you honestly think I'd be such a fool as to tell the motive for them?"

"You wouldn't be a fool. Some form of blackmail—extortion— whatever it was, Millay's type hardly ever are novices. It's perfectly probable that he had a string of victims a mile long. His mother held the purse strings, and my guess is he used his racket under cover from her as a source for ready cash. Whatever that racket was. It would throw the field wide open if you'd tell us, and it would be helpful to you. You can understand how it is? Frankly, that right now you're entered as the favorite?"

"Is this a build-up to a formal arrest?"

"No, Mr. Tyler. It isn't."

"Then I still can't make you out. I will tell you this. Francine has never done a shameful thing in her whole life. That's a fact and it's final. And I think that's all I'm going to say."

And it was all. Henry proved it by the simple process of walking out of the library.

"Well, Miss Gilland," Buran said, "that clears the air of that."

"I'm afraid I agree with Mr. Tyler, Captain Buran. I don't see what the point of it was."

"My point is the same as a doctor's in treating a boil. He brings it to a head. Saves time, I think that the silent, enigmatic cop is old-fashioned and a stupid pose. When you're dealing with sensible people. Mr. Tyler is sensible. Very. And so are you, Miss Gilland."

"Would this be the same sort of a build-up?"

Buran surprised her by smiling with convincing agreeableness.

"No. The Tylers are your clients. You would be just as reticent about any harmful knowledge as he was. And you do have that knowledge, Miss Gilland. I'll skip the rigmarole about suppressing evidence, also about landing you in the lockup as a material witness and then beating your ears back with rubber hoses. With a semi-moron it works. Not you. Anyhow, the shock to Chaney would be indescribable. What I do want is the stuff you will willingly give me."

"On exactly what, Captain Buran?"

"This. Mr. Harden's organization was engaged to look out for the Tylers' interests. Every servant on the plantation knew that—second hand from the Wynstable staff—before Mrs. Tyler left for New York. So everybody knew it. Millay definitely came under the heading of being a

Tyler interest. Naturally you'll have had Mr. Harden look him up. We've started our own line of inquiry in Cleveland, but you're already way ahead of us. What can you tell me about it?"

Margot gave him this: Forrest's soft war berth in the Pentagon through political pressure, the party-machine angle and Pittcairn. Such things would soon be known to him anyhow through his own digging. But no Los Angeles. No Hermosa Beach and Jimmy Smith. Nothing else.

He listened intently. It was, he said, interesting and opened up new patterns. Although it was difficult to see just how a political angle from the past could apply right now. Evidently he thought it silly to picture Forrest in the role of a secret-stuffed henchman engaged in blackmailing Pittcairn and then being silenced by a paid killer. Pittcairn was finished. Nothing would bother him, because he no longer had any position of power to be bothered about.

Curiously, Buran took a sudden side twist: "Do you know what's the key to this whole thing, Miss Gilland? It's the answer to what and who brought Millay here last night to put him on the spot. Detoured him from Charleston."

Patrolman Fleury busted the party up. He loomed in the doorway on the wind of an apologetic cough.

"Want me, Fleury?"

"Please, Captain."

Buran thanked Margot, said they would talk again later, and left. He left her considerably wrecked. Clearly he was hot on the scent of the hold that Forrest had had over Francine, and was juggling blackmail against extortion in his mind. Jake should know this, and right now. To be given the emphasis for haste with the photograph test.

With Fleury again in residence and with Buran around on the loose, she would have to resort to the inn's dial telephone. She set out for the Wynstable along the pathway through the cypress glade.

Its oppressive qualities and funereal mysteriousness closed darkly about her, and unconsciously she quickened her steps. She was halfway along its unnerving desolation when a stranger appeared, coming toward her from around a bend. She thought him either a leftover reporter or else one of Buran's men.

He deliberately blocked the pathway when they met. "Miss Gilland?"

"Yes?"

"I'm Jimmy Smith."

CHAPTER 23

A pair of wood doves sang mournfully behind streamings of Spanish moss while the sun, in its difficult penetration through an over-lace of cypress tops, patterned the path and flecked the acid brown of swamp water.

For a powerless moment while the afternoon hung deadlocked Margot looked at Jimmy Smith. She took in the flashy cheapness of his good looks and dress, saw that his eyes were large and dark and sly, that his lips erased all virility from his face because of their sensitive petulance. An unmanning effect of the apparitional hit her, caused both by the scene's unearthly setting and by Jake having settled Smith so firmly in her mind as being in Mexico.

As a result of this stuporous bewilderment she said, not too brightly: "You're supposed to be down in Guaymas." Smith's grin was perfectly meaningless, just a crack in the lower part of his face under the changeless eyes. "Take another look, babe. Because I'm not."

He talked on with a sort of negligent candor that served to indicate an abundant self-satisfaction as to his mastery over the Tylers and whatever unpleasant fate he held in store for them. Furthermore, it showed a thorough indifference toward any move that the Harden outfit, via babe (nee Miss Gilland), might be silly enough to imagine they could cook up to block him.

He had, he said, taken a Friday-night flight East, having come to the conclusion that he could cash in more heavily here in Parnellton than by any shilly-shally dickering with that Jaffries sketch out in Hollywood.

"You know how it is when you start mulling," he said. "Yes."

"So I asked myself what would Jaffries jack up to. Maybe five grand, maybe even ten, and so what?"

"Not exactly a pittance, Mr. Smith."

"Babe, it depends on the point of view."

"Of course. Buster. And yours?"

He had the natural disinclination of a needler against being needled, and the Buster offended him sharply. For a frightening, and certainly revealing, second his whole expression altered from the aging, pretty-boyish into an unpleasant chart of suspicious malignancy.

His voice changed, too, dropping its burble of young, animal good spirits and sinking its register into a hard sort of pettish vindictiveness.

"Okay, Miss Gilland, we'll play it straight."

"Much better, Mr. Smith."

He had never, he said, trusted Millay fully, but he had been satisfied that Millay would stay in line. Satisfied, that is, until he had received an answer last Thursday to a letter which he had air-mailed Millay.

The letter had concerned Jaffries's snooping and questionings, and Smith evidently had begun to get the wind up. He had felt that things were getting too hot for comfort and wanted Millay to send him the balance of his cut at once.

Millay's reply had not been satisfactory. It included the information that the Harden outfit was working for the Tylers—Margot at the Parnellton end and Jaffries undoubtedly a Harden man covering the coast. As far as any immediate cash was concerned, that, Millay wrote, was impossible.

"In many ways," Smith said, "he was a dope. He had a big-shot complex but his guts were yellow. Can you imagine his signing off with the corny warning that if I fell for any private deal with Jaffries he would have me taken care of permanently?"

The thought of anything so ridiculous restored Smith's inflated egotism and again put him in a good humor. His disturbingly empty smile returned. He told Margot that his original purpose in flying East had been to bypass Forrest and enter into direct negotiations with Melissa Tyler, as it was she, when you came right down to it, who held the dough.

The murder, however, had altered this sensibly forthright plan. With Brandgwyn having become the focus of police attention, it no longer seemed healthy as a base for dickering. And neither were the Tylers, because, unless the cops were hopeless yokels, they equally would be under strict surveillance.

So he had hit upon using Margot as a go-between. He had been on his way just now to get in touch with her, himself in the guise of an out-of-town reporter, in order to arrange a suitable rendezvous for concluding the deal.

"Exactly what is it you have to offer?" Margot asked.

"A negative and several prints. They're dillies. You'll get it when you see one."

"I already have."

This disturbed Smith enough to have him examine it warily for a space.

"I wouldn't think that Francine—"

"She didn't. I found it. And we will clear up one point right now. It's this: the negative and prints are worthless in themselves."

Smith's wariness increased and the feminine weakness in his lips came into full play, giving them the snarling grimace of a rodent sensing a trap.

"What do you mean by in themselves?"

"The picture was faked—the background dubbed in, montage used—that stuff."

Gradually the look of hard, flat concentration left Smith's eyes. He almost laughed. He said with convincing indifference: "That's just your personal opinion. Hang onto it if you like, and see how far it gets you. It changes nothing."

"I must insist that it does. Look here, there would possibly be some value, some cash value, in your admitting how the faking was done and, naturally, in your signing an affidavit to the effect."

"Nuts."

"Mr. Smith—have you considered that the police can establish whether you were here on the spot or whether you were in Charleston last night?"

He looked at her pityingly.

"You're not that dumb, Miss Gilland. Who's to tell them I even exist? You? Me? The last thing either you or the Tylers want is for the police to establish anything about me at all. Use your sense. What good would it have done me to kill Millay? Think it out."

"Yes, I see your point. But the police mightn't."

"That is true. It is why I want this deal handled quick and then get the hell out of here."

"Just what is your asking price?"

"Two hundred thousand."

"For a faked job?"

Suddenly, viciously, his voice lashed out at her: "You can skip that faked stuff. And get a load of this: if a print of that negative gets to the cops, it will hand them the motive. It will pin the job straight on the old man or her mother or on the kid herself. And unless the Tylers fall into line I'll see that the cops get one. Then I'll fade and I'll wait. I'll wait until one of them gets elected and gets fried. I'll still have the negative, Miss Gilland. And I'll leave it to your imagination just how I'll cash in."

"I—shall want time to think this over, Mr. Smith."

"You will get none. What am I supposed to do? Dangle around and suck my thumb in a hot murder situation? Quit kidding yourself and come to."

"I suggest that you come to. A sum of that size isn't picked up in a minute."

"With her dough, it is picked up just when she wants it. Tomorrow is Monday. Tell her to fix it at her bank or her brokers. Tell her just what will happen if there is anything phony about the deal—the cops get a print. I will give her exactly until tomorrow night."

"Mr. Smith, where can I get in touch with you?"

"I will telephone you at three o'clock tomorrow afternoon. We will then go on from there."

CHAPTER 24

The dial telephone booth, just off the Wynstable's lounge, was humid and close. It blurred sweat into Margot's eyes and dimmed her view through the door glass of that section of the room that was visible. It was a view saturated with the inn's inertia, which reached its logiest on a Sunday afternoon.

She was factually clear in the report she gave Jake on Buran's stepped-up drive for the crime's motive and on the severe shock of Smiths phantasmagorical appearance and shakedown proposition.

"He's dangerous," Margot said, "because he's vindictive and essentially weak. You ought to see his mouth. And he's got the Tylers cold. But what he asks is fantastic. He's completely out of bounds."

"No he isn't. That picture, Margot, is not a fake."

It was like getting a belt in the face. It made her sick. Churning sick, of the cold kind that puts a clammy wet coat on the skin. It lasted while Jake told her about it.

He had arranged things right after her morning call so that Jannisworth would be standing by when the manila envelope reached New York. Jannisworth had got to work immediately on the blackmail print. There was no one more expert in the country, and only within the past half hour had he reached his decision that the photograph was genuine and had not been doctored.

There were still the snapshots which Smith had taken of Francine at Hermosa Beach. They were being worked on now by his entire staff, even though Jannisworth considered it a senseless waste of money and of time. But Jake had insisted. And so it looked, he said, as though Smith had them. Melissa Tyler would have to be told and be advised that the wisest, safest course would be to give Smith the money.

"Must we—could I hold back Jannisworth's opinion from her?" Margot asked.

"You're still not convinced?"

"No."

"Even remembering that Jannisworth is considered infallible? That his conclusions have never been questioned?"

"Even so. I won't be satisfied until after the last beach snapshots been tested—and you won't be either, otherwise you wouldn't have kept him at it."

Possibly, Jake admitted, she was right. But only in a wishful, clutching-at-a-straw sense. He agreed that it would be kinder, infinitely kinder, not to let Melissa know that the picture was valid. So far as things stood now, it could do no harm. He would call Brandgwyn as soon as Jannisworth had finished testing the Hermosa Beach snaps—in the hopelessly improbable event that Jannisworth would have reversed his opinion.

When she left the telephone booth Margot found the lounge populated to the extent of one dozing and one dormant convalescent guest, both of whom were arranged in wicker chairs at a window, and by Miss Tishman, who was just leaving the gift counter.

As Margot very definitely was in no mood for a dose of social chit-chat, she set her course toward escape, but Miss Tishman easily succeeded in intercepting her, offering both a pair of sympathetic eyes and a translucent hand of greeting.

"I do hope that Mrs. Tyler is feeling better today, Miss Gilland?"

"She is, thank you, Miss Tishman."

"Last night must have been such a shock to her, especially when added to an illness. I have just made a purchase of several soda mints for Miss Lynndecourt. She finds herself a trifle upset—not because of last night, but because of now. It affects her nerves and they affect her stomach."

The "now" checked Margot from what would have been a polite murmur of sympathy and an immediate leave-taking.

"Has something just happened, Miss Tishman?"

"Oh, nothing *alarming*, Miss Gilland. It's simply that she took upon herself the task of defending Mrs. Millay from the reporters. There are times, so many times, when Miss Lynndecourt will persist in overestimating her strength. Such as that terrible time this spring when the Misses Jellestaby hand-dipped their paisley in naphtha."

Margot left the Jellestaby ladies to their inferential flames and said: "I should think that Captain Buran could have posted a guard to keep reporters away."

"I feel sure he would have, but they didn't appear until after he had gone, and by then it was too late. I declare, Miss Gilland, they kept swarming in like a cloud of vocal locusts."

She emphasized the enormity of this imagery by adding that even dear, calm, little Cloquette became upset enough to produce a quite identifiable bark. Margot continued at anchor, this time by the information that Buran had preceded the grasshopperish newsmen. Evidently just prior to his descent on Brandgwyn, and, as obviously, on business concerning the crime.

"I—don't suppose Mrs. Millay mentioned what she and Captain Buran spoke about? Naturally I'm interested, Miss Tishman."

"Why, of course you are, just as all of us are. And there was no need for Mrs. Millay to tell us a thing, because it just so happened that Miss Lynndecourt and I were relaxing in the patio when Captain Buran called."

The gist of the talk between Buran and Mrs. Millay reduced itself from Miss Tishman's strolling account into two parts. The first had been an insistent effort by Mrs. Millay to be told just when she could arrange for Forrest's funeral. ("It has become an *idée fixe* with her, Miss Gilland, and she talks of little else.") Buran had evaded being specific, but he had held out a tentative possibility that the arrangements could be set in motion reasonably soon.

Then Buran had taken over for Part Two. With a truly remarkable show of patience, and for the greatest length of time, he had attempted to have Mrs. Millay recollect some hint, even some isolated word, which might indicate the reason for Forrest's inexplicable appearance at Brandgwyn's front porch when he should have, instead, been directly on his way toward Charleston.

"The interview was so very much like those psychiatrists one reads about, Miss Gilland. With their patients on couches."

Miss Tishman, who thought the practice revolting, hastily added that Mrs. Millay, although admittedly horizontal, had remained well within the bounds of good taste. She had been stretched (a perfect lady) upon the open-air propriety of her patios chaise longue.

"Was Captain Buran successful, Miss Tishman?"

"No, he wasn't. Mrs. Millay's subconscious remained unpierced. Nothing came up—not the faintest thing that could explain her son's rendezvous with death."

CHAPTER 25

Brandgwyn, when Margot returned, was a house of ghosts. Even the dour Fleury was not in evidence. Nobody was. As her philosophy embraced the sturdy if cold-shock cliché of always taking the bull by the horns, she went straight upstairs and rapped on Melissa's living-room door.

Melissa was alone. She was sitting with a book, unopened, on her lap. Her kindly eyes and smile as she greeted Margot were bleak.

"I'm glad you've come, Miss Gilland. Henry and Francine went for a little drive to take the air. I didn't feel quite up to going with them, and I've been lonely."

"I wish that what I've come to see you about was more pleasant, Mrs. Tyler. It's something which Mr. Harden feels you must know. Although it concerns Francine, I'm just as certain as I know you will be that she personally had nothing to do with it. It's simply that she's been made the victim of an ugly extortion scheme."

Melissa fingered the book for a moment and then said quietly: "Of course I'm certain. I would just as soon believe there was no heaven as to be otherwise. It has to do with that false picture, hasn't it?"

Margot felt almost drenched with relief.

"Then you knew?"

"Oh yes. Henry told me Thursday night, just after Francine had told him about it out in the garden. Henry always tells me everything, Miss Gilland. We have always been very close. I think that my unhappiness at what Francine must have been suffering was what made me ill on Friday. I couldn't share it with her, you see. Henry and I both agreed it would be more than she could bear if she were to know what I knew. Children are so complex, so deeply vulnerable in their hearts. It's best at times to let them think they are sheltering you, rather than for you to shelter them."

"I guess it does give them strength."

"Yes, a certain courage when they need it most. I am going to ask your advice about something, Miss Gilland. I believe you know instinctively how greatly I trust you, and the confidence which I have in your sympathy."

"Completely."

The bleak look grew starker in Melissa's eyes.

"I understand from what Henry has told me that Captain Buran is terribly concerned as to what brought Forrest here last night, and I've been almost distracted over worrying that he might decide either Henry or Francine had been responsible. He might decide so, mightn't he?"

"Yes."

"Neither Henry nor Francine knows anything about this. Again, it's that painful problem of just adding to their worries. But I've been going out of my mind trying to decide whether it would be helpful or harmful for Captain Buran to know about it. You see, it was I, Miss Gilland, who brought Forrest here last night."

It was an impressive jolt, and to a certain extent Margot tried to readjust her blindly intuitive opinion of Melissa, to be sensible about her and regard her clinically and no longer through rose-colored glasses. It was a hard thing to do.

It was all reasonable and believable as Melissa told it, and Margot did her utmost to accept the story at its face value.

She had determined, Melissa said, to take things into her own hands and save Francine from being coerced into marriage. But she had wanted to do so in such a way that Francine would never know that she, Melissa, was aware of the source of the coercion: the false print.

Well, Melissa was satisfied that the primary thing which Forrest had been after was money. So yesterday afternoon, while Francine had been at the Fort Sumter with the Calverses, while Henry had been out walking, while Margot had been in her rooms, and while Sally in her chair by the window had fallen fast asleep, Melissa had gone downstairs and called Forrest up at the Millay cottage.

She had exacted a promise from him that Francine was to know nothing of their conversation. She had asked him to come to Brandgwyn and wait outside on the front porch. He was to reach there shortly after eight, when Francine and Henry would have started for Charleston, when she presumably would be in a drugged sleep from the sleeping pill, and when Sally would be in the servants' quarters having dinner.

"I did not know just then, Miss Gilland, that you were to stay at home instead of accompanying Henry and Francine to the recital."

Melissa had told Forrest there was an offer she wished to make him which would be to his great financial advantage. He had agreed to come.

It had been a bad shock to Melissa when she had found that Margot would be home and would stay in the room with her while Sally dined.

"I've been wondering whether it did not occur to you, Miss Gilland, that I really did not take the sleeping pill. There were times when I had the feeling that you almost suspected."

"Yes, I did. But it was just one of those thoughts, the way you think about everything during a time like this."

"Well, I was afraid that you might have. It made me especially want to have this talk, and tell you, and then ask your advice. I didn't take the pill when I requested you to get the plate of peaches." (The plate of peaches, Margot amended, *plus* the paring knife.) "I took it later."

Melissa had pretended to fall asleep and had felt it the greatest stroke of luck when Margot had left the room. She had waited for a while and then, as Margot did not return, had gone to a window to see whether Forrest were waiting down on the porch.

She had seen his body and had imagined him possibly hurt, but not dead. In panic she had run down and gone outside, had found him dead, and had run back upstairs with heaven knew what confusions and terrors in her mind. "Did you leave the front door standing open?"

"Probably I did. I've no recollection of having closed it. I know I just got into bed and that my nerves went completely to pieces. That was when I took the pill. Should we—must we let Captain Buran know about this, Miss Gilland?"

"I know you don't want to. And I know it isn't for your own sake, Mrs. Tyler, but because of the blackmail print being why you sent for Forrest."

"Yes. I simply could not have spoken. But then I thought I could just pretend that I had decided Forrest was nothing but a fortune hunter, and that I had wanted to prevent the elopement by buying him off. I could take a very firm stand just on that."

Margot chose her words with care.

"Captain Buran also would want to know this—whether you might not have seen something, caught some glimpse of, say, some movement when you were looking down from the window. It's a point he would press, press you strongly about, Mrs. Tyler, no matter how much you tried to convince him that you hadn't."

Tears sprang into Melissa's eyes and then trickled down her cheeks.

"He would think just as you are thinking, but I felt I could make him believe me—that I saw nothing, *nothing* but Forrest, Miss Gilland, and at least he would know that neither Henry nor Francine was responsible for Forrest having come here." The tears thickened, choking up Melissa's voice. "Oh, you see, you do see why I could never talk this over with Henry."

Margot did see, clearly. What shook Melissa were the things which her mind saw, even though her eyes had seen nothing. Henry? Francine? Either would be dreadful beyond bearing. A glimpse of movement of one, of the other, in swift retreat around the road's curve or within the shrubs?

"Don't, please don't cry, Mrs. Tyler. Eventually Captain Buran will have to know of this and of the picture, but there's already been a delay and I don't think any harm will come of it if you delay a little longer." Margot shifted to the therapeutic value of the businesslike. "Tomorrow you will have to arrange to get two hundred thousand dollars in cash. We will need it by tomorrow night."

Bewilderment did check Melissa's crying. Margot explained what the money would be needed for. She touched on the iron control that Jimmy Smith held on the situation. She said nothing of Jannisworth's opinion on the prints validity, hut let Melissa feel that what they were buying would be both the method of the falsification and Smith's exit into silence, his riddance from their lives.

"Can you get the money on such short notice, Mrs. Tyler?"

"Yes, and get more if it should be necessary." Her tears got on the job again, but this time they were the scalding ones of a misery which had been pent up too long, too lonely, in her heart. She said with an abject bitterness: "It's so lovely, when you have little, to dream about sudden riches. But you lose so much when you get them—you lose all the things you had. Oh, let him take all of it, Miss Gilland—all."

CHAPTER 26

Jake's call came through at eleven. Margot had been in the library since dinner, waiting for it and reading, or at least going through the motions of doing so.

The Tylers, after coffee, had excused themselves and gone upstairs. They had gone, as Margot hoped, either to bed or into some tightly knit family huddle with no one knew what depths of mutual clinging and washing away of the secret barriers that had been holding them apart.

They had not, she hoped, gone into a dread-ridden session to plot with amateur strategy how best to save any one of the three of themselves from the legally grim results of Forrest's murder. And yet this legitimate possibility could not be erased from Margot's thoughts. Certainly, she knew, it could never be absent from Buran's.

Fleury, as during the previous night, was holding down his literary post out in the entrance hall. This time the paper covers embraced a romance which in addition to its torrid glow of high passion still managed to work in a couple of very satisfactory stiffs.

Margot took no chances on Fleury's absorption with his book proving any anchorage. She closed the office door and kept her voice low. Jake's own voice had a note of elation. He told her that Jannisworth's estimate of the blackmail picture still stood: it was a perfectly valid job and had not been faked.

But the girl in it was not Francine.

The relief of this left her dizzy, and weights seemed to fall from her as he talked. Jannisworth, he said, had blown the authenticated snapshots which Smith had taken at Hermosa Beach almost up to photomural size, and his proof that the girl in the blackmail print was someone else was conclusive.

It was, Jake said, a fiendishly clever scheme. Hollywood was fallow with "doubles," and Forrest had simply located a double for Francine, unquestionably with Smith's assistance.

"You can see how believable it would be, Margot. Take that series of photo ads running lately, the which-one-is-which? type—which girl is the true, gorgeous Colbert—accept no substitute."

Painting a replica of the tattoo mark on the double's thigh had been simple, and it had naturally helped to clinch the illusion that the girl truly was Francine.

The trick never would have been detected in the negative's original size of 4 x 5 inches. Jake was turning loose his West Coast staff to locate as promptly as they could both the double and the artist who had duplicated the tattooed bust of Washington.

As to just how this would affect the Smith deal, Jake told Margot to keep on playing Smith along. Even if the double and the artist were located before the hour that Smith would designate for the meeting, Margot still was to keep it. Smith still had to be bought off, to prevent him from flying off the handle and contacting the police before he faded.

However, there would now be no need for Melissa Tyler to arrange for any such sum as two hundred thousand. Ten thousand would be plenty to get all that they wanted from Smith. This would be a signed statement covering the fraud, to clip on to Jannisworth's results.

The negative (presuming that Smith actually had it, which Jake doubted) and any prints were to be destroyed. They were now a menace rather than any asset to Smith, because of their proven falsity. They were worth nothing so far as any future gouging of the Tylers was concerned. And they were, on the other hand, tangible evidence of his attempted extortion.

No, Jake said, Smith would most gladly grab the ten thousand as the price for his silent exit. For the job had turned into a stalemate. He would take the money and at once put as much permanent distance as he could between himself and the Parnellton police.

They said good night.

They hung up.

There was no feeling in either of any personal risk being possible to Margot in tomorrow's forthcoming rendezvous. It was a business deal, nothing else. The fangs of the foul picture had been drawn, and the last thing in the world that Smith should want would be to stir up any trouble. It seemed absolutely simple.

* * * *

The killer, fretful, and although lying on a comfortable bed, found no approach to sleep. It would have to be done again. But this time, how? The night wore on, sluggish, warm, without breeze. The killer continued pondering a variety of moves, as though mired in a mental game of unusual chess. The night swung to its darkest moment, then paled, and its stillness splintered hesitantly into bird song. Why not do it as before? Why not follow precisely the blueprint that already had been put to such good use? As thought returned to the simple and very effective steps of Saturday night the killer's breathing slid from its natural evenness into a sound that, as it grew in intensity, resembled the harsh râle of a sick animal. Yes, it had worked out very well before. Yes.

CHAPTER 27

The quiet of Monday morning was a thorough bluff, for beneath it grated a cacophony of nerve ends all of which were loosely exposed in the raw.

After Fleury's bulky departure around seven o'clock Brandgwyn officially was alone, with no visible sign of either the house or the Tylers being under observation. With the exception of the servants (but with them, of course, any variation in lassitude would be imperceptible), nobody had had much if any sleep.

Before having turned in, Margot had gone last night up to Melissa and given her the heartening result of Jannisworth's tests. "I'm so glad, and so terribly appreciative, Miss Gilland," Melissa had said. "If I don't cry it's because your news really isn't any to me. I mean it was simply impossible for Mr. Jannisworth to have come to any other conclusion."

Immediately after breakfast the Tylers left, as a solidified triad, for Charleston to see Melissa's bankers. In the emptied feeling of the house Margot, alone and nervously restless in its closeness, faced with nothing beyond the sapping business of waiting until Smith telephoned at three, tried to put her mind on the job of the day's mail.

She could not. Her sitting room gave her the sense of an oppressive constriction. Its windows were opened on green distances yet they seemed solid barriers composed of the morning's heat. Irrevocably, her thoughts returned to the crime, to the deliberate, continued refusal of the Tylers ever openly to discuss it, themselves to step entirely aside from the picture and speculate on the possible identity of an unknown killer.

Well, had she? Had she herself factually dared to do so any more than they had? She knew very well that the mind could pull tricks such as this, could effect a protective blindness against something you knew was there but did not want to see. Willfully she brought the problem out into the open in its cold, stark little skeleton of common sense.

Of all of them, of the Tylers and surely of the Calverses, Melissa best had known that Forrest would be on the porch at eight. Henry had told her of the blackmail print, told the whole vileness of the extortion scheme, and Melissa would have hated Forrest with a thoroughness impossible to gauge. At her hand had been a weapon, the paring knife. Mothers had killed to protect their children.

Was Buran right? In his contention that the core of the problem lay in who and what had put Forrest on the spot, had detoured him from Charleston? Well, Melissa was that who and what.

Had she told Henry of the meeting which she had arranged with Forrest and of her purpose to try to buy him off? Had she told him in spite of her convincing statement that she had not?

Then, had Henry appreciated the improbability of her success? He hadn't been inactive in his own plans for stopping the elopement, when Margot considered the setup in the swamp cabin with its clothesline, knives, and wall spikes. As for a weapon on hand that night at eight, he could have had a clasp knife in his pocket. Fathers also had killed to protect their children.

Francine?

She would not reasonably have known of the rendezvous nor reasonably have had a knife. However, she would have had her proximity to the scene, her privacy from observation while Henry had been inside the house trying to locate her evening bag. She would have had her loathing, tension, hatred of Forrest and her deadly fear of the print's ever being exposed. And her will to kill. Her fingers around Margot's throat had not been put there in fun.

All right, there the thoughts were, out in the open. Margot could feel no revulsion, certainly no fears beyond a biting concern for the Tylers at the crimes consequences.

And still her skin felt cold now when she thought of Melissa or Henry or Francine as it had not felt cold before. Because so genuinely the force of reason centered the act among those three. You could appreciate the justice of a killing because the appreciation in itself was an academic matter, but the killer was a thing of flesh.

As for anyone else? Except through the nonsense of sheer happenstance, would anyone else have been on the steps of Brandgwyn at eight? The coincidence was farfetched enough to make it seem absurd.

Nevertheless, on the periphery of her mind, very dimly so, were the Calverses. Financial ruin reportedly faced them, and the life belt of the Brandgwyn fortune had been in their grip, only to have been snatched away by Forrest. That setup still had stood valid straight up to the moment of the murder.

Not Anne Calverse, alibied among her fellow committeewomen at the Fort Sumter. But Braintree? He would have been on the loose until the concert curtain at nine, with his arrogance and his attributed violence on a quality with Bruce's. Weakly, he lingered as a possibility.

Far less weakly would be Bruce himself. There was his frustrated passion as a tailor-made incentive plus the convenient blank-out that had seized him well before and long after the hour of eight. Under its amnesic influence the magnet of Brandgwyn, synonymous with Francine, could have drawn him to the porch where Forrest had been waiting. Admittedly Bruce had been carrying a penknife, the one which Buran was having tested for traces of human blood.

Lastly, what about Jimmy Smith? His Friday-night flight East had placed him in Parnellton on Saturday. But Margot saw the answer as a definite No. Money was his objective, nothing else. No hate, no fear, no passion, no revenge. For him to have murdered Forrest would have accomplished nothing except gratuitously to hang a dangerous albatross around his neck. No one but a fool would do such a thing, and whatever else he was, which was plenty, Smith was not a fool.

It was lunch time when Margot put an end to this inconclusive stewing. She ate without appetite in the solitude of the breakfast room, cutting the meal as short as possible, and then went back upstairs. She lay down and succeeded in catching a desultory sort of nap only to be wakened, at two o'clock, by Jarvis. He announced that Mrs. Braintree Calverse was downstairs in the green drawing room and would appreciate it if Miss Gilland would join her. The announcement held a reminiscent, a twice-done ring.

Margot found Anne Calverse a changed woman. Her frothy elegance of costume remained the same—this morning it embraced a pale rose linen with a bonnet of buds in shy bloom—but the social glaze was gone. Her face presented a small mask of tragedy and her eyes held genuine depths of some urgent despair. She wasted no time over formalities.

"Miss Gilland, you must tell me, please, where I can find Francine."

"She drove into Charleston this morning, Mrs. Calverse, with her parents."

"Yes, so Jarvis said. But can you tell me where in Charleston?"

"I'm sorry, no."

"I took the liberty of using the telephone. She is not at Signor Castelaronni's studio. It was a stupid thought, under our circumstances, but my only one. You will forgive this abruptness, Miss Gilland?"

"Of course."

"It's Bruce. This is very difficult to say—it's so personal, so purely a family concern—but then you did see him here yesterday. I'm referring to his condition. He spoke of your kindness."

"I understood thoroughly, Mrs. Calverse."

"The point is that when he reached home after Francine had refused to see him he started to drink again, heavily. I think he kept it up all night.

I doubt whether he slept. I know neither Braintree nor I did. He came downstairs around noon and—well, frankly, Miss Gilland, I'm afraid. I am almost afraid he might harm himself. I'm telling you these intimacies because I'm begging you to help me. Please, *please*, if you know where she is, and for any reason cannot let me know, will you get in touch with her and persuade her to go quickly to Calverse Hall? Will you, Miss Gilland?"

Margot swiftly considered how far she dared go toward reassuring this shaken, frightened woman. With the picture fraud being exposed, that obstacle no longer existed between Francine and Bruce. It seemed certain that there was no other.

But she could not admit to Mrs. Calverse that the Tylers were at the Charleston bank, having gone to it for the delicate, hazardous purpose (if Buran should get wind of it) of drawing ten thousand in cash with which to muzzle an extortionist and forced him to leave town.

"I'll try, Mrs. Calverse. I'll do my best."

The tragic tension of Anne Calverse's expression lessened.

"You are very kind. Very. I love him so, Miss Gilland. I love him so much."

Margot telephoned the bank as soon as Anne Calverse left. They located Francine in the president's office, and Margot explained. Francine said she would have Henry and Melissa drop her off at Calverse Hall on their way home.

CHAPTER 28

The Tylers had not returned by three o'clock, when Jimmy Smith's call came through.

"Mr. Smith?"

"That's right." His voice was in its harsh, irritable register. "Well? Everything settled?"

"It is. Mrs. Tyler is in Charleston arranging matters. There will be no trouble."

"There better hadn't be. Get me straight on that."

"I do. Look, Mr. Smith, the house is no longer under police observation. Why not have our discussion here, and let the principals themselves sit in on it?"

Smith's reception of this notion was explosive. His tone was thickly vicious with suspicion.

"*You* look, and get this! I want no part of that joint or that knife-throwing ape or none of them. You, and you alone by yourself, will meet me when and where I tell you to, and you will have the dough"

"All right. It was just a suggestion. When?"

"Make it at eight."

"Eight."

"Go to a dump called Compton's Tourist Cabins. They're on the coastal highway that passes the plantation gates and are about halfway between you and Parnellton. They're not over a ten-minute walk from where you're standing right now."

"I remember having driven past them, Mr. Smith."

"You will find me in Cabin 10."

Smith hung up.

The afternoon took on an acceleration of speed. At four o'clock Melissa and Henry got back. While they rested in the library for a moment, taking a breather from the heat and their nervous strain during their stop-over at the Calverses where they had left Francine, Margot told them about Smith's message and what the arrangements were for the meeting.

Melissa handed Margot two sealed packages.

"This is the money, Miss Gilland. The smaller package has the ten thousand, in one-hundred-dollar bills. The other has fifty thousand, also in one-hundred-dollar bills. I thought it wiser for you to have at least that much in reserve in case Mr. Smith should become unpleasant and insist on more. And now, if you will both excuse me, I am going to lie down. No—please, Henry—just a little rest until dinnertime."

Margot watched her leave the room. She thought: it is impossible, unthinkable for that woman to be a killer—never Melissa. And Henry watched, with a strange mixture of emotions, but mostly with plain devotion showing in his eyes.

Perhaps it was due to the intimacy of this mutual regard, to Henry's knowledge of its genuineness, which caused him to remark out of a blue sky: "I suppose it has puzzled you how she could ever bring herself to marry me."

Margot was absolutely rocked.

"Well—yes. But not after I came to know you."

Henry's smile was the familiar one, as it had been before Saturday night.

"It's a tough thing to explain. I got this paint job started when I was a kid in Baltimore—clasped hands on my left forearm. No one else in our gang was tattooed and it made a hit, set me apart as something special. I guess it went to my head, like stamp collecting or cocaine. You're smiling?"

"I'm thinking just how big a hit it must have made at home."

"Oh, that was all right. There was no home, not the way you think of one. Anyhow, like a hophead, I kept adding whenever I could afford to—a snake charmer here, a flag or dagger there. I went to sea as a stoker around that time and had ports all over the world to get fussier in, more high-brow, the rarer issues, you might say."

"Like the One Penny Magenta."

"That's right. But with me the tops was the Sinking of the *Maine*—a three-rib job in the middle of the chest. Next I hooked up with the carnies and of course got completely sunk. Melissa—I just don't think I can explain Melissa, Miss Gilland. I guess there are some things that can't be talked about. Almost it's a mistake to try."

Margot went upstairs to bathe and dress. Unconsciously she found herself selecting the darkest silk in her wardrobe: a forest green shot with midnight blue, and for a moment she wondered why. Smith, of course. He so definitely insisted on the clandestine, and this faintly Theda Bara number seemed the most eligible in which to skulk.

Both from a gustatory and a social point of view, dinner was a washout. Francine had called up and left word with Jarvis that she was staying over at Calverse Flail. A footnote added an indication that the surface of love's rocky road was again smoothed over to a pink glacé. Margot had

had no word from Jake. There had been no Buran, and not even Fleury had shown up to take his accustomed post of the past two nights.

"There's one thing I want to do," Henry said after they had left the dining room for the library. "I want to go with you, Miss Gilland."

The time, then, was half-past seven.

"It wouldn't be wise," Margot said.

"I can at least go with you as far as the cabins, and wait out in front."

"No, Smith's attitude over the telephone showed that he's edgier than ever. He sounded as though he'd downed a few shots of nitroglycerin."

"All the more reason why I should be within call."

"I'm afraid I'm putting it badly. There's no possible risk to myself—none—but there could be to the deal. I'd be willing to bet that Smith is hiding outside in the shrubbery right now and watching the front door. He'll want to check up on whether I leave here alone and whether I've a bag with me big enough to hold the money. I've an idea he'll trail me to the cabins just to make certain no one follows me. That's why I don't want you with me. He might easily blow up, and so would the deal."

"Well, when you put it like that. Just the same—how long?"

"Long?"

"Before I go and—well, how long should it take?"

"I see—the Marines—but again, please don't. Smith's not going to be happy when I spring Jannisworth's report on him and then drop the price down to ten thousand. It's bound to take time to bring him to his senses. No—don't do any bursting in even if I'm not back here for an hour, possibly several hours. It's not a deserted-house setup. It's a camp for tourists, and I can't think of anything that is more comparable with a goldfish bowl. So please let it ride."

"All right, I will."

A quarter to eight.

The smaller package of ten thousand dollars went into a summer bag of close-meshed material. The larger package of fifty, Melissa's reserves, offered a problem. It was impossible to conceal it about the slinky dress without, certainly, causing a raising of eyebrows over what would at its kindest appear to be a unique digression from the structural norm. Margot put it on a library table.

"If I do need this," she said, with that unconcern so frequently encountered among famous last words, "I'll come back and get it."

CHAPTER 29

Twilight had not yet deepened to dusk and the mimosa-fragrant air was a touch tempered by the approach of evening from the day's depressing heat.

As she walked along the drive toward the plantation gates Margot resisted her impulse to glance back over her shoulder and take a check on her prediction about Smith's bush-lurking. She could hear no footsteps, but then she would not, as he would follow her in parallel behind the mask of the drive's border.

The coastal highway was empty of traffic, and she had passed the entrance drive to the Wynstable inn before the first car breezed by heading north. Neon lighting, gashing the fading day, came in view. It announced with no restraint whatever that Compton's Tourist Cabins were on the job.

Margot still did not glance behind her for a trailing Smith. Not since childhood had she felt so akin to Fenimore Cooper.

In addition to its cabins, Poke Compton's layout had a main building which housed the office, a bar, a juke box, and a dance floor. The latter was edged with booths in which Southern-fried chicken could, to the everlasting embarrassment of the South, be obtained. The dance floor was popular with the personnel of Parnellton's furniture works and drew a pretty good crowd every night.

There was one thing which Margot had not taken into consideration. This period of the year, June, was out of season. During the fall, the winter, and the spring months the cabins were consistently overflowing into each others laps with occupants en route either to or from the Florida resorts. Right now, however, they were rarely occupied, except by some eccentric tourist or an occasional couple from Charleston with ideas.

The cabins were laid out in a horseshoe pattern. There were twenty of them and, because of the off-seasonal slump, they were unrented with the exception of Number 10. This one was located in the far curve of the horseshoe, which set it a good distance back from both the highway and the main building. A planting of chinaberry trees and of purple bougainvillea around the grounds gave it further seclusion.

As it was too early in the evening for the bar and dance hall to have got into swing, that building seemed equally deserted to Margot when she passed it. Her confidence in the businesslike character of what she was getting into remained sturdy and suffered no letdown from the general air of desertion that verged uncomfortably close on the morbid.

Number 10 was a replica of all the rest. It had an abbreviated front porch on which were two canvas-seat chairs. The door opened into a cubicle foyer. This foyer had three doors, the one in the rear going into a shower room, with those on either side leading to a bedroom.

No lights showed in its windows, but the hesitant twilight made their necessity questionable. Margot knocked, with no result. She then did take a good look back along the curved roadway to see whether Smith had in truth been trailing her. She saw no movement on the road, no stirring among the bougainvillea or the chinaberry trees.

She knocked with more emphasis and the door swung inward. Going a step inside the foyer, she said: "Mr. Smith?"

The shower-room door was shut, as was the one on her right. That to the bedroom at her left stood ajar. One corner of a maple-stained dresser showed through the opening. An ash tray on it held a cigarette, lighted, sending its finger of smoke straight up in the draftless air.

The cigarette indicated that Smith had not, after all, been following her. He was in the cabin. She attributed his silence to an overdose of observant wariness and began to grow impatient about it.

With the subconscious and not particularly brainy notion that by doing so she would convince him that she was alone, Margot went fully into the foyer and shut the front door.

"Mr. Smith?"

With the front door closed, the foyer darkened and the silence of the place seemed absolute. By now thoroughly fed up with being among the last of the Mohicans, Margot opened the left bedroom door further and went inside.

In the dusky light from the room's two windows she saw, successively, a straight-back chair with a pigskin suitcase on its seat—then a hat rack with one of its hooks supporting a snap-brim, sage-green felt—then a double bed with Smith lying on it soaked with blood from a knife wound in his jugular vein and dead.

* * * *

A lathe operator from the furniture works and his girl friend parked their car, went into the dance hall, and selected a booth.

They ordered two beers from Poke Compton, after a dab of polished conversation that had consisted in: "Been hot," "Damned hot," and, as the girl's more refined contribution: "Very hot."

The girl held her hand out for a nickel which she dropped into the juke box wall control, pressing the button for a number sung by Bing Crosby.

Crosby's voice, in diminuendo, drifted out lazily among the chinaberry trees and the purple bougainvillea and in through the open windows of Cabin 10.

Margot stirred.

She had been standing rigid from shock at the wet, red swelter, some gobs of which gave a clown look to Smith's ashy face. Weaving through the glut of her mind were the points: he had been freshly killed, because blood seeped and the cigarette still burned. Pointlessly killed, it seemed.

But that was not necessarily so. If you thought, as she sickly thought, of what had been his conscienceless greed. Had he baited other hooks with the negative and prints to haul in some more of his beloved dough as a tasty icing to Melissa's?

A killer other than one of the Tylers was, without argument, indicated. Without argument? Not literally. For what about Henry? Telling Melissa his intention of following her, Margot, after all. Actually, overtaking and preceding her by a crosscut route. With his knowledge of the time and the spot where Smith would be, and killing Smith with pleasure as the companion bug to Forrest.

A Calverse? To Smith, not knowing of their rumored financial shakiness, they would represent a rich source for his dough. An offer of sale to the infatuated Bruce of the negative and prints—silly, that—silly—

But the negative and prints, had the killer searched and got them? She stirred a bit more from her sweated lethargy and went to the suitcase on the chair. It was unlocked. She raised its lid, to be confronted with the view of a murderous sports shirt, sunset-hued socks, tired linen—no negative, no prints.

But under the surrealist men's wear lay a plain, unsealed envelope.

In it, pasted on a sheet of note paper, was a scrap of printed matter. This had been torn from the page of some book which, judging by the matter's content, had been medical.

The fragment read:

> It is a well-established fact that disease is able to produce the picture of morbid old age prematurely, and in the remarkable but rare condition of progeria—

Progeria?

Where had the word been spoken—said in connection with—

From behind Margot's back came the sound of breathing. It was unlike the sound caused by ordinary breathing. Rather, as it mounted in intensity, it resembled the harsh râle of a sick animal. It could not be Smith's breathing, because he couldn't. Galvanized by utter terror, Margot swerved, and the knife, instead of accomplishing its intention to sever her spinal cord at the base of the brain, gashed the flesh of her neck.

She whirled and saw it, the bloodied little blade, in the lunging hand of Mrs. Millay.

CHAPTER 30

Coincidentally with Margot's having entered Cabin 10, Buran had reached Brandgwyn at eight o'clock.

He was shown by Jarvis into the library, where Henry and Melissa were doing their best to tranquilize a mutual dose of plain mental torture. Although obviously trying to be so, Buran himself was anything but calm. He had come, he said, to see Miss Gilland and had been told by Jarvis that she was not at home.

"Where is she, Mr. Tyler?"

"She went for an after-dinner walk," Henry said. "She takes one every night."

It should be noted that Buran, as yet, had no reason to disbelieve this, that he showed no dereliction either of judgment or duty by not taking immediate steps to retrieve Margot from what he would have recognized as a mission of salient danger.

"A walk around the grounds?"

"Yes. Sometimes it's the gardens or toward the bay. Sometimes even as far as Parnellton for the exercise. Is it important?"

"Yes."

"Could we be of help, Captain Buran?" Melissa asked.

"I don't think so, thank you, Mrs. Tyler. I'm after some information I think Harden uncovered about Millay. He'd have passed it on to Miss Gilland. I need it and I think that now she'll be willing to give it to me."

It was at this point that Buran spotted the package on the library table where Margot had left it. The bank seals, its shape, both were significant.

"So that's why you drove to the bank this morning, Mrs. Tyler. Is the money for Mrs. Millay?"

Melissa was genuinely astonished.

"Why, no. Why ever should it be?"

"Because it could be the reason why she murdered her *son*."

Buran picked up the package and fingered it, almost as though he were trying to press a solution from it to his perplexity.

He said: "About twenty minutes ago I found evidence of her guilt. It's sound evidence. But I *still* hate to swallow the belief that a mother would kill her son, no matter what the pressure. I'm utterly stumped for a conceivable motive. Money? This money?"

Through the granite state of shock in which Melissa and Henry were gripped, faintly from behind the closed office door, the telephone was heard ringing.

Melissa said: "She wouldn't have. She couldn't." Melissa added, to Buran's complete confusion: "Anyhow, she didn't *know*, because Forrest kept it from her. But even if she had known—no, not even then. Captain Buran, you must be mistaken."

He was on the point of assuring her that he couldn't he, when Jarvis came in. Mr. Harden, Jarvis announced through the mud-thick atmosphere, was calling Miss Gilland urgently from New York. He had explained that Miss Gilland presently was out, and Mr. Harden wanted to know where she had gone. He had information for Miss Gilland of extreme importance.

"I'll talk with him," Buran said.

At the telephone, Buran identified himself. He told Jake he had unquestionable evidence pointing to Mrs. Millay as the killer.

He did not mention that she was still at large.

Right then the fact of her freedom was, to Buran, quite logically one of only minor importance. Actually of no importance at all. She was unaware of the two pieces of damning, dumfounding evidence he had discovered when, just now, he had gone to the Millay cottage to tell her that her son's body was officially released, that the funeral arrangements she so avidly had desired could be instituted.

The cottage had been empty, and while waiting for her return he had almost literally unearthed the proof of her guilt. Then a carefully noncommittal inquiry put to Miss Lynndecourt, who, with Miss Tishman, was at dinner in the inn, had informed him that Mrs. Millay had mentioned taking a possible evening walk to the "establishment" (morgue) where her son was. This walk was moistly labeled "pilgrimage" by Miss Tishman.

So Buran was in no sense concerned on the matter of Mrs. Millay's present freedom. There was no earthly way in which she could be aware that her guilt had been exposed, and lacking such knowledge, she would have no reason to be panicked into any brief, futile flight.

He had taken the routine precaution of posting a man at the cottage and having another sent to the mortuary. The arrest would be made when she showed up at either point. Her leisurely and uncharted route between them, with its short furtherance of liberty, was inconsequential. His own tough concern was in piercing the puzzle to the crime's motive.

Therefore, ignoring all these lesser things, Buran repeated to Jake his unwillingness to believe that a mother, unless demented, would kill her son. And Mrs. Millay in no sense could be considered demented. He had been waiting to have a talk with Miss Gilland for possible enlightenment, but now perhaps Harden would give it to him.

At his end of the line Jake swiftly considered. Inasmuch as Jannisworth had exposed the picture fraud, any stigma to his clients, the Tylers, had been blocked. Furthermore, now that the Millay woman was apprehended (Jake unquestioningly took it for granted that she was in custody), the extortion angle would of necessity be brought out during the trial. In spite of the resulting publicity, there was no question but that the sympathies of both the press and the public would rest solidly with the Tylers.

In point of actual time, at this spot in the talk between Harden and Buran, little over half of one minute had been consumed.

Jake made his decision. He capsuled for Buran the extortion angle. He followed this with an abridgment of the thunderclap report that his agent, Davis, had telephoned in during the late afternoon.

Davis, Jake said, as the result of his investigation in Pittcairn's home town, had gone to the village of New Franconia, Michigan, which had been listed on his death certificate as Hillgrove Millay's birthplace—the Hillary who was Forrest's father and who had died ten years ago.

In the village cemetery Davis had located two gravestones. One was a plain slab giving the dates of Hillary Millay's birth and death. The other stone was ornate and showy, and this one gave the dates of the birth and death of Penelope Millay. In addition to which (as a clincher) it was inscribed with an indulgent sentiment as having been erected by her loving son Forrest Millay.

"Then this woman here—she *isn't* his mother?"

"That's right, Captain. I'm coming to that, but there's some more background material you ought to have first."

Several of the older village inhabitants had remembered the Millays well, painting Hillary as having been an erratic, unpleasant drinker who would, it was thought, beat up his wife when under the influence.

Penelope had divorced him and he had left town. (In Forrest's version to Francine this divorce had been listed as a separation.) After Hillary's exit the village knew nothing more about him until, ten years ago, his body had been shipped to a local undertaker for burial in the family plot.

Penelope, with the boy Forrest, had moved to some place in the Adirondacks soon after the divorce. Nothing more was locally known of them until Forrest, a few years ago, had shown up with his mother's body and had had it buried. Forrest had offered no information about the years when he had been gone. He had left right after the funeral, and so far as New Franconia was concerned, it knew nothing further about him and cared less.

Naturally, Jake said to Buran, the hot question now faced them as to who *was* the Penelope Millay convalescing at the Wynstable and posing as Forrest's positively interred mother.

It was curious, Jake said, how a word would occasionally open up some significant train of thought. The word "convalescing" had done so with him. It had recalled to his mind an earlier report of Davis' from Cleveland in which the rental clerk for the Wade Park Manor had mentioned (to Davis) that Mrs. Millay had been shy about entertaining guests because of her appearance: the ravages left by her illness, and that the illness had sounded to the clerk as something like "delayed progeria."

"It registered such a total blank with me, Captain, that I looked the disease up."

Jake had found it to be a malady that aged the looks of a person far beyond his years. So much so that a person although in reality young would show all the more devastating appearances of age. He had even gone into it more deeply and had telephoned his doctor. His doctor had confirmed the matter, adding that although progeria almost entirely was confined to children there were so few case histories of it on record that it was entirely conceivable that a more mature person could contract it.

So there they were. The Mrs. Millay of Cleveland's Wade Park Manor and of the Wynstable inn was a far younger woman than she looked. Even apart from the evidence offered by the gravestone in New Franconia, she could not possibly be Forrest's mother. As a matter of fact, she was probably younger than he.

The elapsed time in the talk between Harden and Buran was, at this moment, just under four minutes.

"And so it's your baby, Captain, from that point on. Just who and what the woman is is up to you. Incidentally, what put you wise to her?"

"Duck bones."

"I'm afraid this connection—"

No, Buran said, the connection was all right. The break, when it came, had involved a duck.

His laboratory men, he told Jake, had identified some foreign specks in the contusion on the back of Millay's skull as being minute particles of velvet, even to having established their original color as a citron green. Also, they had identified a very faint trace of lipstick on the cigar, which of course indicated that it could have been lighted by a woman.

Buran again stressed his never having for one instant considered Mrs. Millay as a suspect, because apart from her careful alibi (ordering dinner sent to the patio—Walter removing the empty dishes—Miss Lynndecourt and Miss Tishman chatting with her from the time when Walter took the tray away), there was that damnable subconscious refusal to consider any mother killing her child.

Instead he had been attributing the velvet particles and the lipstick either to Francine or Melissa Tyler, less seriously to Anne Calverse, and with practically no seriousness at all to some hypothetical local girl who might have had good cause and intent to jab Millay in his throat.

This evening, just prior to reaching Brandgwyn a few minutes back, he had gone to tell Mrs. Millay that arrangements for Forrest's funeral could now be made. He had found her cottage empty, a fact that in itself had been a little puzzling.

While he had been standing in the patio waiting for Mrs. Millay to show up, Miss Lynndecourt's pug, Cloquette, had wandered over. His own movements, Buran said, must have waked the awful animal from the post-supper nap to which she was addicted.

To his astonishment, the slug suddenly had exhibited enough life to start digging in the earth of a flower border. Buran said he had observed, for want of anything else to do, what was being uncovered. They were a few bones, with the flesh still on them, from a roast duckling.

His thought process from then on had been academic.

Mrs. Millay had ordered roast duckling Saturday night, the murder night. Her alibi rested entirely on the twenty-odd minutes when, in complete privacy, she presumably had been eating a dinner of roast duckling. A game knife would have been part of the cutler service for roast duckling.

Knowing then clearly what he would be looking for, he had given the cottage another search. Inside a citron-green velvet evening bag of the drawstring type were traces of sand. Filled tightly with damp sand and then swung, the bag would have—and Buran said he was satisfied that it had—made a workmanlike weapon for the blow that had knocked Forrest unconscious.

"But as I've told you," Buran concluded, "the motive floored me. So I came right here to see Miss Gilland. I felt she would now be willing to talk, since the Tylers no longer were implicated."

"You came—let me get this straight, Captain—do you mean that Mrs. Millay had not returned to the cottage when you left? She is not under arrest?"

No, Buran said, she was not. He briefly explained his lack of concern.

Jake, in New York, turned cold.

In a tense voice he told Buran of Margot's scheduled rendezvous with Jimmy Smith. He told him just how Smith fitted into the picture. He frankly admitted the proposed dicker between the Tylers and Smith.

He pointed out that Smith, in addition to his planned shakedown of the Tylers, could easily have been aiming a shakedown at Mrs. Millay as well—a thought that could explain her true destination on having left the cottage. For certainly any pilgrimage to the body of a son who wasn't a son was balderdash.

And the most unpleasant probability of all: Smith would not know that Mrs. Millay was a killer.

Nor would Margot.

CHAPTER 31

The blade descended, entered flesh, and its point on being withdrawn was followed by blood. The silence of Cabin 10 was no more than negligibly disturbed from Margot's slow, loose slump to the bedroom floor.

Whether Miss Gilland were dead or not could be determined in the following minute or two, Mrs. Millay decided, better than at the urgent present.

A corner of the sheet of note paper with its pasted-on fragment of medical information covering progeria showed on the floor from beneath Miss Gilland's left shoulder. Mrs. Millay eased it out, but in spite of her care two fingertips touched blood. She reminded herself to wash it off in the shower room before leaving. Also, of course, the knife.

Mrs. Millay checked the time by her wrist watch, moving nearer to a window, because of the evening's quickening approach, to get a better look.

It was her intention to be found resting on the patio chaise longue (a spiritual and physical wreck from her mortuary jaunt) when Miss Lynndecourt and Miss Tishman returned to their cottage from dinner. An added poignancy would color her exhaustion through herself being dinnerless, having given room service orders that none be sent over because of her suitably appetiteless state.

Seven minutes after eight.

So there was no over-excessive pressure for haste, and certainly none at the expense of the least carelessness. Using the knife, she slit the lining of the suitcase, and under it, as she had expected, were half a dozen prints of the blackmail picture. These she tore into small pieces and managed, after several flushings, to get them down the drain.

She did this because to her, as with Smith, they presented a menace in their obvious role of motive. While it, motive, remained an enigma to the police she felt comfortable in her certainty that the Tylers would move heaven and earth to prevent its exposure. Later on there would be good financial possibilities in the negative, which at the present was secured in a safety-deposit box listed under her maiden name of Edna Cantling in Cleveland.

Mrs. Millay's reasoning was perfectly valid, when you considered that she knew nothing of Jannisworth's exposure of the fraud. But it did offer an interesting example of the "slip" made by most criminals. In this instance a mental one.

Margot was a Harden agent, and Harden as a matter of course would be as aware of the blackmail print as Margot was. From Mrs. Millay's warped viewpoint, a sufficient slice of the Brandgwyn fortune easily could buy his silence where a murdered Forrest and a murdered Smith were involved. But the least use of common sense would have shown Mrs. Millay, if the whole angle had not completely slipped by her, that Harden never could be silenced if handed a dead Margot.

She completed her business in the shower room by tearing up the sheet of note paper with its progeria clipping and watching the pieces swirl drainward on the first flush.

And now, she decided, she was ready for Miss Gilland.

As Mrs. Millay took hold of it Margot's pulse was slow, weak, but perfectly in evidence. She released the wrist and, studying the slumped body, anatomically considered points of entrance for the knife, while knowing perfectly well it would end up by being the same old jugular vein.

In reality this pause was serving Mrs. Millay as a rather needed moment of emotional rest. During it the black streak which in the room's twilight was blood reminded her of her stained fingertips and, in turn, of fingerprints, and thence to the lining of the suitcase, which she had gripped while ripping it loose.

The demands for a little haste were beginning to accumulate, so with a touch of impatience Mrs. Millay left Margot and tried to detect any blood marks on the cloth.

The ceiling light would help, hut to turn it on was naturally out of the question.

Becoming thoroughly exasperated, she used the knife to slice out the ripped section of the lining and shoved the cloth down under the neck of her dress, wanting to waste no further time with drains, where in any case the material would cause a block.

Again she was ready for Miss Gilland, but once more, moving to a window, she checked the time and discovered with an unpleasant annoyance that it *was* thirteen minutes after eight.

The window at which Mrs. Millay was standing had its shade raised above the level of her eyes, and she could see the roadway for some distance along either side of the horseshoe curve. She realized that what had caused her to look at the left-hand road were the driving lights of a leisurely approaching automobile.

This automobile was a 1941 model sedan. In addition to an overflow of luggage, clothing-on-hangers, and sundry cardboard boxes, it was occupied by an elderly couple, their daughter and son-in-law, and a small girl of around six. They were en route from Paterson, New Jersey, to Haines City, Florida, to take over a modest business property recently inherited.

They had been on the road all day in the blistering heat and were tired out, dirty, and, in their several fashions, irascible from general irritation. Poke Compton, standing on the running board, directed them to a halt before Cabin 12, where, he told them, they wouldn't feel lonesome—it being but one removed from Cabin 10, in which a young fellow name of Martin, from Idaho (this was the alias Smith had chosen), was stopping, and they could get neighborly if they liked.

From between uniformly gritted teeth they said that they didn't like, so Compton gave them the cabin key and walked back toward the dance hall and his bartending.

Rather than any shattering fright either at being discovered awash, as she was, in her bloodletting or at the good possibility of being trapped until black night would cloak her, Mrs. Millay's first reaction to this out-of-the-blue incursion was one of intense annoyance. It was bound to delay her exit until they were unpacked and settled inside the cabin, unless she wanted to depart under full view of their eyes, which would be fatal.

From the crouched position she had taken at the window she caught the glances directed toward Cabin 10 when Compton pointed it out as a target for social exchanges. This brought Mrs. Millay carefully upright, and she went to the foyer and turned the key in the front door, which was the cabin's only door, as an elementary precaution against any inspirational visiting.

The key was of the ordinary house type, having no qualities of precision manufacture whatever, and thanks to its absent-minded relationship with the lock in which it operated, the twist which Mrs. Millay gave it in her anger caused it to jam.

This caused her a wrench of fear. But it was instantly effaced with a confidence that wiggling the key would loose it (such keys had not been uncommon in her past), and in any event, the sills of the cabin windows, with their removable screens, were a scant four feet above the ground.

She wasted no time with any immediate wiggling but returned to her observation post where, again crouched down, the activities of her temporary jailers compellingly absorbed her undivided attention.

The old lady, obviously at the end of her physical rope as well as her patience, was occupying one of the two porch chairs and looked permanent. It was a position from which she inescapably commanded a direct view of Cabin 10's door. The old gentleman was pickingly advising the young man about what to unload from the car and what not to unload, this to the young man's rumblingly mumbled displeasure.

The young woman and the child had gone inside, and the child's name was Agnes: a trivial bit of useless enlightenment determined by Mrs. Millay from the mother's voice, querulous through the open windows, saying: "Agnes dear,—please—please for Mother's sake, Agnes, will you for God's sake shut up?"

Mrs. Millay examined her watch. The time was sixteen minutes after eight, and any thought of now making the Wynstable before the Misses Lynndecourt and Tishman were finished dining was absurd. But did it seriously matter? Not really. Her sad wending to the mortuary and back would have taken a little longer, that would be all.

Then slowly, through her powerful absorption in her besiegers' doings and this quirk at the passage of time, Mrs. Millay experienced her first dose of true alarm as she recognized with what perfect clarity sound carried in the evening quiet. The voices of the two men, even the voice of Agnes's mother from within, to say nothing of Agnes's own piping contributions, each had been brilliantly clear.

She looked thoughtfully toward the dark corner but could detect no stir, not a murmur of breathing, and she speculated whether Miss Gilland were, without the need for further assistance, dead. The darkness of the corner lessened as her eyes corrected the slender variance in their focus from the outdoor twilight, and it seemed to Mrs. Millay that the patch of flooring which should have contained Miss Gilland was bare.

It was bare.

A dissection of this interesting phenomenon would come later, when the head-stuffing marrow of its devilish potentialities would lessen. Mrs. Millay stepped softly through the open doorway into the foyer, which also was bare.

The front door key remained as she had left it, jammed. It was all very curious. She had heard no sound, but would she have? The faint, and possibly quite silent, movement of Miss Gilland sliding herself along the floor? While her own ears and eyes had been spitted in their attention on the voices and potterings of the tourists?

Angrily Mrs. Millay quit this unthrifty line of untimely musing—the fact stood out that she hadn't. She had heard nothing connected with Miss Gilland while Miss Gilland had been slithering herself to wherever it was she was now.

Both the door to the second bedroom and the one to the shower were shut. Mrs. Millay examined the bedroom first because of the availability of its windows for escape—the window in the shower room being high up, square, much too uncomfortably proportioned to be clambered through by anybody, and completely ridiculous for a person so weakened from shock and loss of blood, so lightly threaded to life, as was Miss Gilland.

While pondering this weakening, Miss Gilland, it seemed, had still had enough physical reserves of strength for movement. This presupposed a state of consciousness, and therefore a capability to hear the tourists talking, so why hadn't she screamed for help? This was swiftly resolved. Miss Gilland must have realized that at the least whimper out of her, she, Mrs. Millay, would have struck.

The bedroom was empty, even under its bed, and its window screens were undisturbed.

Mrs. Millay returned to the foyer. The shower room seemed so headless. But then, having so curt a journey left her to dribble into death that the remaining gap scarcely mattered, Miss Gilland might well be headless. Was it the front door key being jammed? Thus barring Miss Gilland from its use? Had it forced her into the course of least resistance—yes, Mrs. Millay remembered she had left the shower-room door standing open after having flushed the papers.

Mrs. Millay turned its knob and gently pressed.

The door did not give even slightly. Its inside bolt, a solid, three-inch sort, had been shot home. Mrs. Millay drew in a deep, shuddering breath. What a clever thing for Miss Gilland to have done. But why, so secured now against any *coup de grâce*, wasn't she screaming for that help which lolled just two cottages away?

How idle! Miss Gilland wasn't screaming for the simple reason that she couldn't. Otherwise she would be. Her tatters of strength had been precisely limited to getting her into the shower room's haven, to inch her fingers upward so that they might bolt its door. Then total loss of consciousness. A syncope drowsing toward the grave.

Mrs. Millay's breathing annoyingly retained its freshly acquired mannerism of shuddering. She went into the bedroom occupied by Smith's soaked body and once more over to the window for a crouching look. The scene had changed. The unloading of the car was either completed or else at a temporary halt.

Agnes's mother and Agnes had joined the others. They were sitting around on the porch and grass, lazy over a picnic supper from the contents of a paper bag and two cardboard shoe boxes.

Mrs. Millay's chest began to hurt from a hot effect of congestion. She lifted Smith's suitcase from its supporting chair, placed it on the floor, and then sat down. It made it easier to think.

The tourists could be solved. The rear bedroom window and a retreat through the chinaberry trees, masked from the tourists by the cabin and their preoccupation over hard-boiled eggs and meat-paste sandwiches, would be the answer.

But there was the budgeless question of Miss Gilland, who seemed so occasionally recuperative.

To leave her here with the sketchiest chance of her remaining alive and hence vocal would be, Mrs. Millay knew, simply signing her own death warrant. She brushed aside the folly of forcing open the shower-room door. In the first place, any attempt at it would raise a wood-splintering racket that would bring the alfresco lunchers over on the run. But if there were some silent solution to the enigma, one that would insure an infallible extinction of Miss Gilland—such as—

Fire?

CHAPTER 32

Poke Compton's office was little more than a large cupboard adjacent to the bar. It contained a roll-top desk, a couple of questionable chairs, and an electric wall clock designed to resemble a frying pan. The hands of this clock were now accurately registering twenty-two minutes after eight.

Packed into the room's stale stuffiness were Buran, Henry, and six of Buran's men who had been alerted by telephone from Brandgwyn and ordered to get to Compton's quietly—no sirens, not even a use of the interrupted-red-lights.

Buran's problem, as he saw it, was as nasty, as delicately tricky a one as you could face. Nothing about it was positive to work on beyond the fact of Miss Gilland's danger. As a result the situation had to be assumed at its possible worst.

Mrs. Millay was its dynamite. He had been able during the brief time lapse since the telephone talk with Harden to have men swiftly cover the route between the Wynstable and the mortuary. No sign of Mrs. Millay.

It was a reasonable enough clincher that she was in Cabin 10. The temperament of any killer was a hair-trigger proposition. With a woman it was worse, because its unpredictability was absolute. On being trapped they might do anything from peacefully busting into tears to going straight off the button and mopping up anyone within reach, as Smith and Miss Gilland were within reach.

Smith was no easy answer either. According to Tyler, Miss Gilland had described him as being badly nerved up. Any blackmailer under any condition of nerves was a viciously tough hazard. No matter what the ruggedness of their exterior, essentially they were epicene, having the characteristics of both sexes and with a craven weakness in their stuffing.

Any rough stuff, any door-smashing frontal attack with such a pair was out. It would mean curtains for Miss Gilland. He explained these things tersely to the men. He added that there was the risk to the new occupants in Cabin 12 also to he considered—two men, two women, and a child.

"So this," he said, "is what we'll do."

CHAPTER 33

How difficult it was to start a fire. A really good fire that would burn a building down not just piece by piece but all at one time and with, in particular, Miss Gilland in it. (Smith's body was of no concern, he no longer being vocal.) Mrs. Millay, in the deepening tones of evening and with a tiresome continuation of her new mode of heavy breathing, examined futility.

A window curtain held incendiary value, but you couldn't run around with a lighted match, even granting there might be some matches, from curtain to curtain rapidly enough to effect a simultaneous result. And nothing short of one would do any good. The first flare—the first puff of smoke—and the diners would cry Fire. The flicker would be doused out with a bucket of water.

Mattresses and bedding just smoldered. It was the fumes that suffocated you when you fell asleep with a lighted cigarette in your fingers, which would drop, and then long before the tardy flames you died from the fumes—asleep—so tired, so strangely, suddenly tired in her head.

Mrs. Millay dug back among the years and resurrected a French word which it had pleased her to shriek startlingly at droopy playmates: *Avant*! She did so over to the window and crouched. They still ate. Her wearying, indignant eyes turned away from the glutting, having been attracted by the appearance of Poke Compton lazily strolling from around the left-hand roadway's curve.

The eaters also were interested, even to a banana bogging itself down in little Agnes's stuffed mouth. Mrs. Millay's lassitude vanished beneath a sharp speculation as to Compton's purpose.

He came to a placid stop at Cabin 12, and Mrs. Millay heard him say casually: "I see you folks are eating."

As this flashy bit of deduction evoked no comment, Compton went on: "Sort of felt you might have thought it was too late for us to serve supper, but it ain't."

"We happen to have a sufficiency with us, thank you," Agnes's mother said in a tone of tasteful formality.

"Yes, ma'am, so I see, and mighty appetizing." Compton's eye lingered on Agnes, who was again under steam with the banana. He took a handkerchief from a hip pocket of his dungarees and wiped a brow that was, even granting the evening heat, curiously heavy with sweat.

"Maybe the young one, maybe all you folks might care to top it off with a dish of good cold ice cream along with a good cold drink of soda pop or maybe beer?"

This rang a gong-sized bell with Agnes, who piped piercingly: "I want ice cream Mama can I have some ice cream Mama I want ice cream I'm hot Mama I want some now Mama—"

"Shut up, dear," Mama said quietly. "We'll see."

Compton gently released a pent-up breath, and his brow, although so recently mopped, was beading over again. "Tell you what, folks—this being your first trip South, guess it's up to me to show you some of that Southern hospitality for which we're mighty famous."

An expressive Paterson, New Jersey, noise which would have felt perfectly at home in the Bronx slipped out of Agnes's father's lips.

Compton blandly hurdled it and said, with an almost too forceful, too persuasive cordiality: "Tell you, now—you ladies look a mite too tuckered from your long, hot, tedious day to do any walking. If you'll just step into your car and if you, sir, care to run us down to the cafe, I'd be mighty proud to have you folks be my guests for dessert."

"After which nickel's worth of ice cream," Agnes's father said coldly, "we will be expected to sit there feeding the juke box and buying out the joint for the rest of the night."

It was the grandmother who took care of that. She said in a thin but compellingly authoritative voice: "I will ask you, Wilfred, to attend to your manners. Different climes, different customs. My son-in-law, Mr. Compton, is scratchy from being overtired. We appreciate your hospitality very much and are pleased to accept."

To plug up any further bon mots from Wilfred, the old lady promptly stood up and walked over to the car. Mrs. Millay watched her get in, watched them all get in, watched the carload of them slowly, miraculously, incredibly, roll around the roadway bend and out of view. Of Cottage 10. Of her.

This reprieve from observation, with its sudden, its absolute aloneness, lifted Mrs. Millay's spirits with the force of some powerful stimulant. So strong was her fever of relief that she felt herself again in complete mastery over her fate. Nothing, now, was lost.

Her watch showed twenty minutes of nine. The Misses Lynndecourt and Tishman would have returned to their cottage from the inn dining room, but what of it? She herself was able now to walk openly out of this trap—no longer a deathtrap so far as she herself was concerned—and in ten minutes be—

Remembrance of Miss Gilland pole-axed Mrs. Millay back to facts.

Rigid, and with her breathing provokingly labored, she stood in appalled wonder over how *could* Miss Gilland have slipped her mind. Then a thought of amazing solace burst in her head like a beautiful rocket: with the troupe from Cabin 12 now well out of earshot, there was no danger left in noise.

Terrifically vitalized by this precious knowledge, Mrs. Millay went into the dark foyer and, feeling so secure, so exhilarated in her mind, blessed privacy, snapped on its ceiling light. Then she critically studied the shower-room door.

This door was a stock, cheap, four-panel job built of pine. Its panels measured a thickness of one quarter of an inch. Mrs. Millay tapped an experimental finger against the upper left-hand panel, which, once smashed, would give easy access to the inside bolt.

The knife with which earlier she had been so busied was a jackknife model. It had belonged to Forrest, and one of its virtues was that its blade, when snapped open, was held rigid until released through pressure on a push button set in the haft.

She plunged the blade against the panel and was gratified over the ease with which its keen steel sank through the soft pine. She worked the blade free. To cut an opening would take too long, but a good blow or two with something would splinter the panel, and the noise could now be safely risked.

An oblique thought came fleetingly that this was especially true because little Agnes, without much strain on anyone's credulity, could be counted on already to have instigated a musical hell via the dance hall's juke box. Yes, now that Mrs. Millay listened for it, she heard the faint groanings of a male voice frightfully backed by the atonality of some sister singers.

Finding a suitable object with which to strike the panel was the first step in order, and so clearly now were Mrs. Millay's wits clicking that they promptly recalled a dresser lamp in the unoccupied bedroom. She had noticed it when she had gone in to locate the then-evaporated Miss Gilland.

The base of this lamp was eight inches in height and molded out of cast iron in the shape of a bloated candlestick. Mrs. Millay removed its pink taffeta shade, unscrewed the bulb, and pulled out the floor plug.

Four blows against the door panel did the trick.

Mrs. Millay looked through the splintered gap. Enough twilight entered the shower-room window to show her Miss Gilland lumped loosely at the foot of the washbasin, possibly in a condition of traumatic shock, possibly dead.

Unmentionably relieved and satisfied, Mrs. Millay slid a hand through the hole, and her fingers, in the fashion of pale, clever demons, groped for the bolt.

CHAPTER 34

No matter how courteously a person might stretch his imagination he would never be deluded into mistaking Poke Compton's establishment as a hangout for the county's elegants.

Under less abnormal circumstances the presence in its dance hall of Braintree and Anne Calverse, Bruce, Melissa and Francine Tyler, Dr. Artemus Ruddage, and the county's district attorney, Alberstoke Chaney, would have, for once, rendered Charleston's society editors speechless.

Melissa had found it emotionally impossible to stay put in Brandgwyn and wait for reports on the state of Margot's security or danger. She had wanted to go just as closely to the scene as she could get, to be right on hand, as near as they would let her be to that friend who for her and for Henry and for Francine was shut in with a trigger-happy (Buran's words) blackmailer and a murderess.

She had telephoned Calverse Flail on the heels of Buran's and Henry's whip-like departure from Brandgwyn, telling Francine how things were, giving her the blessed news that suspicion of murder was lifted from the family and the anything-but-blessed news about Margot's danger. Francine had insisted that she and the Calverses would hurry to Compton's, too, and would pick Melissa up on the way.

Then she had telephoned Dr. Ruddage so that he also might be on hand, just in case.

Chaney's presence among the group was the result of a call given him by the desk sergeant at headquarters. Chaney again was a blissfully contented man. In fact, if it hadn't been for the appropriately measured concern which he set aside for Miss Gilland's dead-duck role in its abattoir background, he would have been an all but openly exuberant one.

The relief—the incalculable relief—on his having learned it wasn't a Tyler or a Calverse whom he would have to speed with his forensics into a murderer's grave but, instead, a locally unpopular and politically non-dangerous Millay went to his head like wine. A woman defendant, true (he docketed the phrase for future use), but at soul a fiend in dastardly possession of that gentle sex. Once more the governor's chair took sharp focus in his handsome, blue, hankering eye.

"I wonder," Melissa said to the patrolman stationed at the dance-hall door, "whether Dr. Ruddage and I might not walk back a ways among the cabins?"

"Sorry, ma'am. Captain's orders. Nobody leaves this joint until the job out there is done."

The patrolman nodded to the special waitress who had been assigned the job of feeding nickels into the juke box, which had stopped. She put some in, jamming down the selection keys at random. An appearance of business as usual had been one of Buran's orders too.

CHAPTER 35

The bolt slide was set rather tight in its stop. This tightness was due to the shower-room door having shifted a bit off its true setting under the four battering-ram smacks which had splintered its panel, and Mrs. Millay's fingers were finding a thoroughly exasperating amount of difficulty over loosening the bolt.

For a while it had seemed as though it simply would not budge, but just now it had given a little and with a torturing reluctance it was beginning to slide. Her breathing once more was intensifying into that harsh, sick, râle sound, while her desperate exertions with the bolt were filming a gummy coat of sweat across her skin.

It was free.

She opened the door. And at last, within a step or two of her knife, most suitably vulnerable, through the betrayal of coma, to a studied attack (there would be no botching the job this time), was Miss Gilland.

Buran's fingers closed around her wrist.

"Just drop the knife," he said.

The shock of this was so strong that it reacted not only on Mrs. Millay's heart but against the nerve centers of her brain, throwing her for an indeterminate moment into a partial paralysis.

Her security against interruption had seemed inviolate, even to the key remaining jammed in the locked front door. The notion that anyone could get in through a bedroom window with almost the same ease with which she had considered getting out of one had never entered her head.

What had floored her hardest was that moment of initial contact when the fingers had closed on her wrist and she had identified them as a spectral Jimmy Smith's.

An unspeakable revulsion at the impossible thought had all but cut her down with its creepish horror.

Buran tested Margot's pulse. He loosened the key, unlocked and opened the front door. Henry and three policemen were grouped before the porch. The other men of the detail were still on guard at the rear and sides of the cabin.

"She's alive," Buran said.

He sent a man to the dance hall to phone for an ambulance and the coroner. Neither he nor Henry knew of Melissa's group, of Dr. Ruddage, having been cut off from any communication because of the necessary stealth of their mission.

He told another man to come inside, then detailed the others to protect the cottage against the curious and himself against interruption. Mrs. Millay, he believed, was in that psychological state of shock when she might make an immediate statement.

Henry stepped past Mrs. Millay in the foyer, not looking at her except obliquely, not wanting to, the trappings of being a human having left her as she stood like an automaton with her terrible breathing. He knelt beside Margot in the shower room.

Buran said: "I wouldn't—"

"No. I won't touch her."

"The doctor—sometimes it's harmful."

"Yes. I'll just sit here."

Buran went into the unoccupied bedroom and snapped on its ceiling lights. He drew down the shades of its two windows.

"Will you come in here, please, Mrs. Millay?"

He caught (Buran knew it was nonsense even as he thought it) a delicate graveyard smell as she brushed past him.

He closed the door.

CHAPTER 36

"What was the relationship between you and Forrest, Mrs. Millay?"

"I was his wife."

"Your maiden name?"

"Edna Cantling."

"Tell me how you met—where—the general background."

"I was acting in summer stock in an Adirondack resort near Loon Lake. You know the kind of setup—giddy rich outlanders, quaint sterling locals. It was near the Corning estate. They still called it that even after Forrest's mother inherited it when Corning died. When he very suddenly died. I was young. And beautiful. Can you imagine it? Like a flower, one press notice called me. I'm still young. Young—young—"

Buran kept his eyes on his notes. Down from the young face so travestied, so old.

"Was his mother living when you met Forrest?"

"Yes, but she was ill. Too ill to go to the wedding."

"Seriously ill?"

"She was on her deathbed, as a matter of fact. I used to relieve the night nurse at times. I was alone with her on the last night. It's when she told me. She was delirious, of course. Terribly. Does that sort of thing frighten you? Delirium, I mean?"

"I guess it would. Never ran into it."

"Well, she thought she was talking to Forrest, that I was Forrest, and she wanted to tell him before she died. She knew it all right, even in her delirium, that she wasn't going to live, I mean. So she wanted Forrest to know where she had hidden the arsenic container."

"She—had poisoned Mr. Corning? You emphasized the suddenness of his death."

"No. Forrest had. It wasn't gastroenteritis, as the doctor had diagnosed it. Forrest poisoned him with arsenic trioxide. The symptoms are pretty much the same, and the doctor was a local old duck."

"About the container—"

"You see, she thought he had done it but she wasn't sure. Not until she happened to find the container. It still held some arsenic and there were fingerprint smudges on it. It was shoved down among the socks in his dresser. Forrest used to drink himself senseless at times and never remembered what he'd done with things. Naturally the night he handed Corning the button he was steamed. She kept it. She hid it."

"The container?"

"Yes, and I couldn't figure out why for a while. Then I decided it was conscience. She couldn't bring herself to the point of turning him in. She was his mother. But her conscience wouldn't let her destroy the evidence. She was strong on church."

"Did you tell him where she said she had put it?"

"No. I got it myself. I kept it. I hid it."

"I see."

"Of course you do. It's perfectly obvious. Do you know about progeria?"

"Yes."

"Stupid of me. You must know a lot of things, you and Harden—and—Miss—Gilland—"

Buran drew her back carefully.

"I suppose that Forrest, when the effects of progeria set in—"

"Certainly. He always was a fool. I knew it when I married him, but I thought at least he was a rich one. Naturally he wanted to divorce me when—you see, my looks—like now—"

"You refused?"

"Of course I refused. I was washed up in the theater. And he had his uses."

"The Pittcairn business? It was you who planned the schemes?"

"Yes. I've said he had no brains. Just looks."

"I take it that your having the arsenic container kept him in line?"

"It did. Also, he began to appreciate me, to feel he needed me as a manager. I mean, for instance, to figure new angles out after Pittcairn blew up in our face—like the idea of using a 'double' in the pictures. That was mine. Do you know, it's funny how patly some things turn out, Captain Buran. We were on the coast and had only pulled the 'double' business on a couple of movie half-bigs when the publicity about the Tylers and the Brandgwyn fortune broke. Of course then—"

"Of course." Buran kept his tone strictly conversational. "Just why did you kill Forrest, Mrs. Millay? I'm not so dumb as to imagine it was from jealousy."

"As a matter of fact—I don't know whether this will strike you as funny or not, but I killed him in self-defense."

"No, not funny—but not quite clear—"

"Well, it would be if you had known him better. As intimately as I knew him. The trouble with the Tyler business was that it was too big. Too big for him. I could tell when it started going to his head."

"I'm sorry, but I still don't—"

"Look. It's really very simple. I hate the phrase, as a phrase, but it's the only one—"

"What phrase?"

"The old double-cross. The scheme was to get her cold through a marriage. You must remember that the estate wasn't settled when the Tylers landed here, so we knew Mrs. Tyler couldn't begin to get her hands on the sort of money we were after. But the marriage would tie Francine up, and we could then put the hooks in after the estate business was finished."

"Mrs. Tyler came into control of the money just before she went north to New York."

"I know, and that's it. When the double-cross began to show. I became convinced of it. That instead of our cashing in right after the marriage and getting out, what Forrest actually was planning to do in his own inflated head was simply to stay on with Francine as the husband of a great heiress—all very proper and reformed. The black past dead, nonexistent. That stuff. It's so comfortable to reform when you're sitting on twenty million dollars. And Francine would have had to put up with it because of the pictures. The catch, of course—but surely you must see it? That the marriage would have been bigamous?"

"Yes, and you the obstacle."

"That's exactly the point. And not only bigamy, remember, but I had the arsenic container as well. Why, of course he was planning to kill me. I could tell it in a hundred little ways. He'd have had to. He killed Corning for gain—so why not murder me for security? And for freedom too? He never did care about my dominating him, and once he had the Tyler fortune under his belt he wouldn't have needed my brains any longer—or me—my—"

"It was too late, naturally, to make him call the marriage off? Just stick to a straight extortion?"

"Much. Nothing could have. I made one stupid attempt—sent a stupid anonymous note to Melissa Tyler to tip her off after Forrest sprang the elopement angle. I knew it was stupidly useless even while sending it. He was beginning to dope out his own moves, getting very sure of himself, really. So when he set Saturday night for the elopement—well, it became my deadline. He'd be married and then he'd kill me. And that was why I had to kill him first, so he couldn't."

"Mrs. Millay, just what did take him to Brandgwyn that night at eight?"

"Melissa Tyler telephoned the cottage during the afternoon. She made the appointment. He told me about it and said she was so vague about just what she had in mind that it worried him. So he decided to keep it and see. Well, then—then I—"

"No need, Mrs. Millay. Later we'll go into it, not now. Of course Jimmy Smith got in touch with you?" The transition was artlessly smooth. "I imagine he wanted to put the pressure on you, too, as well as the Tylers. Get everything he could."

"Well, no. It was a different angle than with the Tylers. You see, while we were in Los Angeles, Jimmy found out about the progeria. From something Forrest let slip one night when they were together. Drinking, of course. Jimmy looked it up in a medical book. He tore the article out and kept it—showed it to me last night when he came to the cottage."

"Was it his bargaining point?"

"It was scarcely what you'd call bargaining. My best safeguard in killing Forrest lay in everyone believing I was his mother. Well, I could scarcely let Jimmy keep the clipping, keep threatening me with his knowledge."

"But just what was it he did want? Money?"

"Of course money, but not right then. He knew Forrest and I spent everything we made almost as fast as we made it. But he also knew I'd have to keep on making a living. So he told me that each time I planned anything in the future he would expect his cut. Well, naturally—"

"Yes. Now there's just this, Mrs. Millay. Tonight, when you came here, you couldn't have known about his appointment with Miss Gilland?"

"No, Jimmy had said nothing about it. I came at eight because those two old wrecks in the next cottage would be at the inn eating. Otherwise, when I said I might go for a walk, they'd have insisted on coming with me. It was like Saturday night with Forrest—same alibi, sort of—same, well, pattern—there is something in that sticking to a pattern, isn't there?"

"Yes."

"You can understand what a shock it was to me when—You see, I'd just started to look for the progeria clipping and the prints when there was that ghastly knocking on the door. Stupidly, very stupidly, the door hadn't been locked, and I knew that whoever was knocking would open it. And then, I mean after having been panicked into hiding in the shower room—I mean when I came out of it and saw Miss Gilland reading the progeria clipping—Captain Buran, aren't they moving something? Out in the foyer?"

"The stretcher. Plasma—transfusions—Miss Gilland will have to be hospitalized."

Curious, Buran thought, the way Miss Gilland's name seemed to react on Mrs. Millay. He wondered why. Why it should do so in special. Obviously more so than either Forrest's or Smith's, both of whom she had so thoroughly slaughtered. Not that it mattered. He had everything they needed now. But it was funny—he looked up sharply—it was funny the way she was breathing. You could call it râle-like.

"Mrs. Millay!"

She caught herself and then said quietly enough: "Don't worry, Captain Buran. I can recognize a last-act curtain when I see one."

This was not her only theatricalism of the moment. Because when Buran opened the door to tell a man to take her and have her booked, Mrs. Millay found herself face to face with Henry, where he stood in the foyer beside Melissa.

For an extraordinary second Mrs. Millay stood perfectly still while her eyes, in peculiar concentration, took him in. In a sense (it was thought later) it was as though she were looking into some form of mirror, as if it were herself she was seeing—not in reflection hut directly with Henry, in Henry, with his carnival-midway tattooing and her own warping side-show grotesquerie of flowering-youth-under-ravaging-age. A joke that made them one and set them apart from ordinary people. It was only as she moved to pass him that she spoke.

"Detestable freak!"

CHAPTER 37

Not much of the evening twilight was left as Melissa walked from Cabin 10 to their car with Henry. They did not take the road but went beneath the chinaberry trees, surrounded by their clean, pungent scent. Her hand rested in Henry's arm and it was very comforting to both of them.

The others weren't going to the hospital. Francine had wanted to, but Melissa had said no—to take Bruce and Anne and Mr. Calverse back to wait at Brandgwyn and she would telephone them as soon as the hospital people decided how Margot was.

It turned out that Margot, although requiring hospitalization for several days, was all right.

Mrs. Millay's initial slash from behind, diverted by Margot's swerve, had done little damage beyond a surface lesion on the neck. The second lunge, after Margot had turned around, had been better. With it, Mrs. Millay had been able to register a stab wound which, although superficial, had successfully effected Margot's weakening loss of blood and state of shock.

One of the curious sidelights of Mrs. Millay's active evening lay in its major casualty (excepting Smith, who was a total one and so not fair to be counted) turning out to be Mrs. Effingdon Frosher.

Bestowing the Wynstable's accolade of residence on the Tylers had been bad enough. The murder of a Wynstable guest had been tougher. But when the said guest's mother turned out not only not to be his mother but very definitely his murderer and then went on with an afterthought liberty of adding another corpse named Smith to her bag it was too much.

As a result of all this, Mrs. Frosher's period of hospitalization exceeded Margot's by a good two weeks, and never, afterward, was she considered to be quite the woman she once had been.

Bruce and Francine were married at Brandgwyn in August.

And in December, one midnight, under the due process of law and the haunted eyes of those required to watch it, Mrs. Millay died.

www.ingramcontent.com/pod-product-compliance
Lightning Source LLC
Chambersburg PA
CBHW022027170626
46808CB00003B/1090